The
End
of the Sentence

SCIENCE
FICTION

The End of the Sentence

MARIA DAHVANA HEADLEY
& KAT HOWARD

SUBTERRANEAN PRESS 2014

First Edition

ISBN
978-1-59606-679-3

Subterranean Press
PO Box 190106
Burton, MI 48519

subterraneanpress.com

For the horned & the hooved, the detailed devils,
& the unphotographable
or
For the monsters.

1.

There used to be a woman who lived at my house. She's gone now. When I got here, nobody'd lived here in years. They'd given me the key to the padlock and so I took the Greyhound. There was a little town, but it wasn't much, a mile of paved road in the middle of dirt. A hardware store, a diner, a gas station. I walked five miles in the heat, because there weren't any taxis and nobody I wanted to ask to drive me from the drop off. People were already acting like they were noticing me, and I felt nervous. I could see them in the window of the diner, and in the hardware store, looking out.

I'd bought the house in an online auction, sight unseen, repossessed due to negligence, city selling it. The house cost $3000. It came with a bone-silver paintless Chevy that didn't run.

It was what I could afford, almost nothing, but this was the kind of nothing you might do something with. The place, in the picture I saw online, reminded me of my grandparents' house in Louisiana. It had shutters, hanging crooked, and a little porch.

When I saw my house for the first time it was the beginning of October and still up near ninety degrees. High grass all up around the walkway, and I made a note to cut that down so it wouldn't catch fire. I felt good about that, like I'd learned some things. I pictured a fence, some green grass, some flowers and then a swingset and a little boy swinging, but I didn't have a little boy. I didn't have much but the backpack I was carrying, and the jeans I was wearing. I'd lost some things along the way. I was thirty-eight when I got to that house. I'd had a whole life before this one.

Wooden, weather-stripped paint, and a flap in the front door for the mail. I looked at the house and felt sad for it. It'd been yellow. There was a tree stump from a tree that had been big. A bathtub in the front yard. Nothing growing. Too long with nobody watching over it. Somebody next door'd had a meth lab which had burned up. It was still a black rectangle. The place looked country, and it was, but it was the kind of country that could kill you.

I unlocked the padlock, unfastened the chain, and pushed at the door. It stuck, like something was behind it, pushing back, and I hesitated for a second. What if someone really was in there, living there? A squatter?

"Hello?" I called out, feeling stupid. I thought I'd know if there was someone there.

I shoved one more time, hard, and the door sighed and budged. Mail, that was all. A pile of it, all over the rucked up floorboards, stretching down the entry hall in an overflow. Hundreds of envelopes. Some yellowing, some newer.

At first I thought it was going to be collection notices, junk, used cars and cable TV, but they were all the same, long white envelopes with handwritten addresses in slanted handwriting. They were all addressed to the same person:

OLIVIA WEYLAND
57 Snakebite Road
Ione, OR 97843

The return address was for the Federal Prison two hundred miles away in Salem, and the pre-printing on the envelope said, *Correspondence From an Inmate.* Each letter was red-stamped *Approved.*

I held one in my hand for a minute, and then put it down in the same spot I'd picked it up from. None of my business, I thought. I'd heard some people had a fetish for corresponding with prisoners. Maybe that'd been Olivia, whoever she was. I had a packet of hotdogs in my backpack. I picked my way over the envelopes, went into the kitchen, turned the knobs, established no electricity. I slung my bag down on the ground, squatted on my heels, took the hot-dogs out, and ate one raw. I needed to eat them or cook them, and there was no cooking, though for a second I thought about a bonfire, all those letters. Too hot. Too dry. It'd be a stupid move.

The house was still full of furniture, if furniture was what you'd call it. Mouse-raddled upholstery, wooden chairs with splitting seats. Broken cups in the kitchen. A plate rail. A table with a boomerang Formica top, like my grandparents' place again. There were bad stains on the floorboards, things that'd need scrubbing and sanding. I thought about pouring shiny varnish over the wood until it shone. I'd once seen a squirrel preserved that way.

I climbed the stairs carefully. One, two, delicate half weight, like that would help me if they all fell down. Dust on them so thick that each of my footprints was clearly visible. There was graffiti on the wall in the bedroom, and it stopped me for a second. Red paint, a diagram of some kind, arrows and lines tagged there by a kid, probably. Wallpaper peeling on the other walls.

It'd need work, I'd known that much, but it was mine. On the nightstand, there was a Mason jar, and in it, flowers, yellow and red twists of velvet. Cockscomb. I always thought they looked like brains. I looked at them for a moment, pleased, before I realized they shouldn't be there. The place had been locked up for months.

The water in the jar was unclouded. Maybe the neighbor, I thought, or the auctioneer, but everything else was dusty.

I thought about the letters filling the hall.

I thought about them some more. They made me uneasy, and I couldn't say why, except that there were way too many of them. A thousand, I thought. I was just at the point of going down and shoving them into a garbage of some kind, when I heard the door rattle.

The sound of the flap being lifted. Another letter fell through the slot. The slap of the flap closing. Nothing else. No footsteps. No car. I looked out the window. No one.

I went downstairs. Only one set of footprints on the treads, mine going up, and now down again. Whoever had left the flowers upstairs hadn't left any marks going up. I felt queasy, then corrected myself. Maybe the conditions in the room were so dry that the flowers only seemed fresh. I was tired. I'd been traveling a while.

I walked over the letters until I got to the door. I bent over, and then jolted back. The newest letter on the floor had my name on it.

MALCOLM MAYS
57 Snakebite Road
Ione, OR 97843

I flipped the letter, my neck prickling, and saw one word, carefully inscribed on the back of the envelope in a kind of calligraphy, embossed with little creatures, leaves and branches:

Welcome.

2.

Tenth October

My Dear Malcolm,

I trust you're settling into the old homestead. There will be a plate set out for you in the icebox, and flowers beside the bed. In the absence of the home- owner, things have been put in place. It is harder these days than it once was, to tend to these matters from afar. The homeowner is only absent, you must under- stand. Not gone. The end of the sentence approaches, Malcolm, and when it comes, I will return.

Of course, you can't know who addresses you, and with such familiarity. No one will have told you of my plight, nor of the years spent in this lonely place. Olivia will not have mentioned it.

No, I have lost time.

Olivia will not be there. When you arrive there'll be no such thing as the lovely Olivia, not any longer. Nor any of the rest of them. Never mind. Never mind the inheritance, the family, the promises. No one will have passed it to you in whispers, no one will have given you your choices.

What is gone is gone, and you are what remains. You're left to me and I to you.

My name is Dusha Chuchonnyhoof, and you will not have heard of me. I'm forgotten everywhere but the hallway where you stand, and the prison from which I write this. It's been years since I've seen the sun, and years since I've tasted the rain. They guard me. I hear their feet, and smell their sweat, but I don't see them. They keep me to myself.

I walked to the window and looked out over the dusty yard. Tumbleweed and a stump of a tree that had already been old when it was cut down, and now was much older, the dead wood splitting and silver. I could see the rings in the stump from here. It was twice as wide round as my arms held in a hoop.

It's been years since I sat in the shade of the old fruit tree that stands outside the windows you look out now.

The End of the Sentence

Sweat dropped onto the letter, blurring the ink. Yellow legal pad. I wanted to crumple it, but it seemed crazy to think I could be scared by paper. Was I scared? My heart was beating faster, but it wasn't fear. It felt like something else. Like, I realized with some surprise, love. This felt like a love letter in my hands, almost a pulse in it. I was dizzy.

I went into the kitchen and opened the refrigerator. The kind with curved metal handles and the freezer on top. Pink with copper shelves. Frost hung in the air as I held the door open.

There was a plate of food. More than a plate. A roasted turkey, sliced partially into sandwich-sized cuts. A loaf of homemade bread, still in its metal baking pan. A jar of fancy French mustard, which was clearly out of my price range. A head of red-edged lettuce, the kind I'd never even look at in a grocery store. A dish of tomatoes. A shaker of salt. A pitcher of what seemed to be lemonade. A fruit salad with slices of citrus and strawberries. A whole coconut cake. There was a bottle of wine there too, with a hand-written label, illegible. A shaky, but elegant handwriting. I shut the door, trembling.

This was supposed to be my house. No one had said anything about an owner. I'd just spent nearly every cent I had on it. This was all I owned, and what if I didn't own it?

I thought about calling the police, but I didn't want police around, not after what I'd come from, and what could I tell them? That someone had said, in a letter, that they owned my house? That there was food in my refrigerator?

I looked to the side of the fridge, and there was the cord, frayed, and not plugged into any outlet. I opened the door again. Cold.

I didn't feel alone. The house felt occupied, but I spun, and no one. Paranoid, Malcolm, no sleep since Kansas.

I stepped again into the entryway. I thought about taking my pack and running back down the road to town, the bus, but I didn't have enough money to buy a ticket, and I had nowhere to go. Everything in my life was gone. I opened my hand and uncrumpled the letter.

Here I stay, one hundred and seventeen years after my capture, waiting for release. My sentence was two lifetimes and a day, for the lives they say I took, but I didn't commit that crime.

And your crime? Did you commit a crime, Malcolm? Are you running from something? I can help you. Your son is not gone. There is hope.

I rely on you now, Malcolm. You're my own, as has been everyone who has lived in my house.

With anticipation,

Dusha

The End of the Sentence

I held my knees and pressed my back against the wall, feeling the house shake with me. There was a sound in the kitchen. The opening of the refrigerator door. The opening of a cupboard. Haunted. My house was haunted. I didn't look up. I didn't move. I shut my eyes and listened to liquid pouring into glass.

When I opened my eyes again, some time later, there was a glass of pale, yellow wine beside me, and a note in that same shaky hand.

Drink.

3.

I drank.

The wine was cold, crisp with an edge that razored along my tongue, a faint breath of slate-grey stone in the glass. It soothed the roughness in my throat. I drank again, deeper this time, and there was the warmth of honey beneath the mineral brightness of the wine.

Dusha Chuchonnyhoof. Neither were names I recognized. They hadn't appeared on any of the forms I'd signed to make this house mine. It was mine, no matter what the letter had said.

(You're my own, as has been everyone who has lived in my house.)

I drank a third time, draining the glass, and felt the house exhale around me. I blew out a breath, too. I did not want a haunted house, but I felt weary of panic, weary of pain. If there were ghosts, I would let them move about in peace for now.

The letters, though, that immense crumbling heap of them. They'd come from a prison. Dusha Chuchonnyhoof, whoever he or she was, was in jail, and clearly—I looked again at the ink on the yellow paper—insane. No one could survive one hundred and seventeen years. Someone was playing a joke. Or if they really did come from the prison, I shouldn't be bothered by it. You could write to whomever you wanted to write to, or so I thought. I'd never gotten a letter from a prison before, but I'd seen it on TV, people writing their way out of their cells, scavenging names and addresses from phone books. My name was a matter of property record. Someone could have it. It was possible.

The letter was unnerving, but mostly because of the manner of its arrival. If I hadn't been here when it slid through the flap, I probably wouldn't ever have noticed it. Perhaps they were all the same, ramblings of the mad person who had nothing but time and a supply of prison paper.

I'd read one. I closed my eyes as I reached into the pile and plucked out an envelope.

Back in the kitchen, an entire meal had been set out for me: a turkey sandwich, sliced on the diagonal and set on a plate, next to a bowl heaped with fruit salad.

The End of the Sentence

"Hello?" I said to the air, but no one responded. "Whoever you are. It's fine if you're a ghost. I've been through some things, and ghosts don't bother me."

No movement.

The glass that stood next to the plate was full of lemonade, not wine, but that was fine. The card, next to the napkin, that read *"Eat,"* was somewhat less fine, but not my concern at the moment. I was made of every kind of worry, every kind of unknown, and it came to me that I'd gotten too hot walking from town. I drank a sip of lemonade. Yes. I was thirsty. And the lemonade was real. As was the food. As was the way the house seemed to be providing me with all I needed.

I opened the letter.

Fourth March

Olivia,

> *Enough. Enough.*
> *You may keep silence, and punish me for whatever wrong you think I have done, whatever hurt you believe you've suffered. That is, of course, your prerogative, and I cannot alter your thoughts.*
> *But the time is coming, Olivia, and steps must be taken. You must be the one to take them.*

You need not write for me to know that you are ill. The house tells me you suffer. But your end does not end the responsibility of the house and those who live in it. The end of the sentence is almost here, Olivia, and when it arrives, I must return.

Tomato dropped from my forgotten sandwich to stain the paper. I wiped the seeds with the edge of my palm, smearing the ink.

I can do nothing else. You know this. I belong to the land, as once I belonged to other land. This land is my claim, and I am vowed to it, and to the family.
Do not neglect your duty, Olivia.
I will not neglect mine.

Dusha.

Not, then, a collection of near-identical ramblings. Not that at all.

I choked down the rest of the sandwich. It was better food than I had eaten in weeks, but I could barely make myself swallow. The fruit salad I scraped back into the bowl in the refrigerator, and I stacked my dishes in the sink.

I gathered some of the piled letters from the front hallway, and climbed the stairs with them heaped in my arms.

The End of the Sentence

The dust gritted under my feet, and the third step from the top sighed loudly as my weight rested on it.

There were linens on the bed. Smooth white cotton, ironed crisp, and scented with lavender. I shook my head. The sheets must have been on the bed before. I'd need to paint over that graffiti on the wall as soon as I could get paint to do it. The design pulled the eye and then didn't let it go, like some sort of gate. No wonder I hadn't noticed white sheets. I didn't picture what I wanted to picture, an invisible someone shaking the sheets out, tucking them in. I'd told the ghost, or whatever it was, that I didn't mind it. I didn't. There were worse things in the world. Never mind that I'd never seen a ghost before, or felt one in my presence. I was at a point of exhaustion where I didn't care about what was real and what was not.

I heard the sound of the mail flap being lifted and closed, and an envelope falling to the floor below.

I would not look.

4.

I set about making the house my own. In the bleary October heat, I hauled out what was broken beyond repair, stacking it in heaps in and around the bathtub out front. Once I was a bit more settled in the area, I'd figure out where the dump was. But for now, best to have it out of the house. It felt like progress. I was being responsible.

The house—*my* house—had clearly been lived in a long time. There were the broken and faded things, yes. Mismatched plastic dishes, pasteboard furniture, chipped jelly jars. But there was also a set of dishes I was pretty sure were real Wedgwood, and a desk of beautiful golden pine that looked to be hand-carved.

Inside the desk were more letters. The same long white envelopes, the same *Approved* stamped in red ink on the outside. These, though, had been opened, read, and bound together in order of date of correspondence. I wondered if Olivia had ever written back.

My fingers left streaks of grime and dust across the envelopes. I heard the screech of a faucet, long unturned, and then the thumping splash of water into a tub.

The tub was clawfoot, a white curtain strung on iron rings hiding the end of it, and half-full of steaming water when I walked into the bathroom. Written on the fogged-over mirror, one word:

Bathe.

I hesitated, but whatever it was in the house with me had been benign so far. Much easier to poison me than to drown me in the tub, despite the horror movie I was suddenly viewing on repeat inside my head. Drowning was hard. The house didn't feel angry. It felt full of something quieter than anger, anticipation rather than rage. There was a clean kitchen, and a gleaming tub. Whatever ghost or ghosts lived in my house, it was a tidy one. The longer I stood there, the more I could feel the grime and cobwebs on my skin. I stripped, and lowered myself into the water.

When I stepped out, there were clean towels waiting, and a pair of old-fashioned men's pajamas, thin blue pin stripes running down white cotton. They were slightly frayed at cuff and collar, but soft and comfortable. My jeans and t-shirt were nowhere to be seen.

I paused at the door. "Um. Thank you."

Sconces had been lit against the darkness of the hall-way, flickering orange light that might have been candles, or might have been some bulb, clever enough not only to counterfeit flame but also to shine without electricity. I looked at the sconces for a moment, wondering who'd installed them. In the half-light, the fixtures looked like hands, though I hadn't thought so during the day.

A storm had come in while I bathed, painting the sky in streaks of purple. Burnt ozone hung in the air like some-one had walked the property, smoking menthols. Thunder echoed in the distance.

The sheets had been folded back, and the letters piled into stacks by the bed. I opened one.

Seventeenth June

My dear Olivia,

By now someone will have told you, though the traditions are not as they were meant to be. The town will have told you of the pair of lovers, and of the blood, and all of the things that I have been found guilty of doing to them behind the great iron door.

The house will have given you the key.
The prison will have told you the date of my return.

We belong now, to each other, Olivia, and so I feel that I can say to you that I did not do the things of which I have been accused, and found guilty, and served one lifetime in atonement of already. There are appeals, and the process continues. They say I will be released. There is no proof of crime.

I will tell you, Olivia, the truth, if you wish it.

I will return, regardless. The house will have told you that you have no choice in the matter, being bound by blood and vow. I would tell you that I am sorry for this, but I will not lie. The truth becomes a large thing, when one is imprisoned for a falsehood.

Take care of my house, Olivia, and it shall take care of you.

Yours, waiting,

Dusha.

My dreams that night were not comforting.

5.

In the night, awakened by the sound of letters falling in the hall, I rifled through the desk in the bedroom. Something insisted I look there. Top drawer, beneath the drawer liner. How quickly I'd grown used to envelopes filling every passage, to a house feeding me and putting me to sleep like a child. I thought it possible I might still be dreaming on the bus from Louisiana, jostled among suitcases and other sleepers. The envelope I found wasn't sealed, and it was different from the rest. Not a prison stationery, this one, but something finer.

January 12th, 1956

Dear Mr. or Mrs. Dusha Chuchonnyhoof:

There is no one of any of those names at this address. No one named Marvel. No one named Eugene. My dear husband Paul is recently deceased, and if you're looking for him, you should consider your manners and respect my time of grieving.

I've telephoned the prison. Your appeals have been overturned. They said it was my duty to tolerate and provide comfort to prisoners if I could, and I shall not tolerate your correspondence. I'm a Christian woman. Though I find myself reduced in circumstances, I do not deserve this torment in addition to my bereavement.

The people next door aren't nice people, and perhaps they're the ones you're looking for. I'm not the type of woman who gets letters from a prison, and I DO NOT APPRECIATE YOUR CHEEK.

I will not do what you demanded in your last letter, nor will I do what the letters sent by your pranksters ask me to do. I'm not a Weyland but for marriage. I'm a Jones from Reno.

~~I'm told you're to go to the gas chamber, and good riddance. I don't know why they've not sent you there yet. Whatever crime you committed, the time you've spent there means it was something terrible~~

I will pray for your soul and that is all.

The End of the Sentence

~~Yours,~~

~~Yours truly,~~

~~Your own,~~

The letter ended with a jagged line of ink, deeply scored into the page.

It was handwritten, in stationery embossed at the top with the name Mrs. Paul Weyland, and an address crossed out at the bottom, and replaced, by hand, with this one. At the very bottom, a smashed insect, a mosquito there sixty years. I shook the paper and watched the dust crumble, then turned my head to look at the graffiti arrow tagged from the bedroom doorway to the rectangle painted on the wall.

A door, it suddenly occurred to me, and then I wished it hadn't. This one wasn't iron. This was only paint.

But it was a rendering of a door, with a crude star-shaped knob. I touched it with my fingertips, and felt the edge of the paint. Enameled. I resolved to go into town to buy some clean white latex to cover the thing over the next day. I had a little money. Enough for that.

Nothing in the house protested or directed me. Silence, but for the arrival of letters, one every few hours. I moved around the bedroom, looking at the door that wasn't a door, and at last, I slept again, dreaming of a prison, everyone in it wearing black and gray stripes, a gas chamber deep in a maze of corridors. I dreamed toward sunup of Mrs. Paul Weyland. "Yours, Yours truly, Your own." It made me nervous, that thought, that someone here might have forced her into such a promise.

Letters arrived all night, rattling the door in such a way that I got used to it, just as I'd begun to get used to everything else, the bed, the food, the bath. I didn't read any more of them.

Bad dreams bleeding into the sunrise. My brain was dull with broken sleep and things I'd seen in movies. (What door? Where was it? Was it on my property? Did I have the key? I didn't want to have anything more to hide. I kept thinking about my mother, and how I hadn't talked to her in a year. Only one person had this address and that person was in prison.)

I stacked the new letters in a patterned basket I'd found in the front hall closet. I had a memory of something like it seen in a book, Native crafts, Western exploration, willow branches woven and pigment-dyed red and black, and for a moment, I had a good association, touching the inside of the basket, of a happy baby sleeping inside it.

Maybe not sleeping.

Suddenly the empty basket felt filled with stones. I put it down, nauseated. I was sweating again, and outside, it was still too hot for the calendar. A glass of water had appeared beside me. I drank it.

The End of the Sentence

Then the feeling of wrongness was gone, and it was just the letters, the growing pile addressed to

My Dear Malcolm.

I wasn't reading them. I cleaned some more, outside this time. A pair of overalls, paint-stained, but washed, had appeared, hanging from the bathroom door. They weren't modern, but nothing was. Like all the things the house had given me, they fit.

I'd found a rusty push mower, and shoved it along the property, then raked up the dry grasses to the best of my ability. Around the edge of the house, the grass had begun to grow in green, and beside the front door, there was suddenly a patch of violets, out of season, and one of mint.

I hauled another load of mess out, TV tray tables, though there was no television, a cracked rubber doll, a rusted bit of metal that I couldn't identify. A branding iron, I thought suddenly. A crude letter C, placed between what seemed to be two swords.

Chuchonnyhoof, I thought, with a sick lurch, looking out at the dry grass, seeing smoke in the distance, not so far off. It came from the place where the meth house had burned, maybe leftovers from some underground flame. Something was on fire there, and I felt lucky it wasn't me.

I ran my fingers over the rust on the brand. Red, and hot. I put it down in the pile of grass, then picked it up a moment later when the grass began to smolder. Frantic stamping on the incipient flames, and I got it out, but I didn't know what to do with the branding iron. I looked at the patch of mint, and at the dampness of the leaves there, and finally, I put the brand into them, relieved as I heard it hiss a C into the soil. The smell of crushed mint and smoke, and I remembered for an agonizing moment my old life, a glass of ice, bourbon, mint, sugar, my wife smiling at me, her face lit up with love. A sunset. Trees dark and tall. Fireflies starting to blink on and off around the edge of the yard, her hand in mine.

That was over and done. "Over and done," I repeated to myself as I walked the property line, "over and done, Malcolm."

Something echoed and I stopped. I turned and looked at the house, at the open front door, the staircase inside it like the bridge of a nose, the upstairs windows like eyes, the porch like a mouth.

I looked at the mark the brand had made, and realized it wasn't swords at all, but a C atop a W.

Olivia Weyland. Dusha Chuchonnyhoof. W & C.

I thought about the smell of branding. I didn't really know what it smelt like. I didn't want to know what might be branded with such an iron.

The sound of something scraping on glass. I turned, hoping to see it happening, a ghost in action, but no, I never did. On the front window of the dead car, traced in the dirt, there was a word.

Drive.

Oh, Malcolm. Malcolm, Malcolm. I didn't want to drive. Didn't want to think about being behind the wheel of anything. That was why I'd taken the bus cross-country. I couldn't drive anymore.

Drive, the word appeared again, and this time I watched it being written, letter by letter, slowly.

I found myself going into the house. I got the ring of keys, opened the car door, and put the key into the ignition, expecting nothing. They'd told me it didn't run. A junker, they'd said, thrown in for the scrap. I'd imagined there was no motor, or what was there was under the hood, rust and mess, but the car started. The Chevy looked like a skeleton, the interior all springs and split leather, a swallow's nest against the ceiling, wefted into what remained of the fabric lining. I looked for a moment at the nest, and then reached up and slipped my hand into the hollow beside it, where an envelope waited.

Twenty-second October

My Dear Malcolm,

In the town there is a small library. I am certain you'll wish to verify the history, the crimes, the accusations. My trial was much covered in the papers.

Yours,

Dusha.

Inside the envelope, there was something else. I drew it out hesitantly. A photo. A little boy, grinning, one tooth missing. Yellow t-shirt.

My little boy. I pressed myself back against the hot leather of the seat, wondering how Dusha had gotten this photo. I'd never seen it before.

But no. No, of course not. This wasn't him. Row hadn't gotten this old. He'd died when he was four, across the country, nowhere near here. This boy must be six or seven. This was the Row I'd imagine when I wanted to punish myself, the Row that wouldn't be.

I stared at the photo. I turned it over. Dusha's writing.

If you do as I tell you to do, he will return when I do. If you do not, he will remain where you left him.

The End of the Sentence

I know your dreams, Malcolm, just as I know the
dreams of everyone who sleeps in my house.

On the dust of the dashboard, the word *Drive*, again.
There was no choice. I drove toward town.

6.

I didn't see anyone else when I walked into the Ione Public Library. Dusha Chuchonnyhoof: a unique name. I figured I could discover the basics from an internet search, rather than needing a librarian. This was my problem, not anyone else's.

One of the chair's casters squeaked as I pulled it closer to the computer desk, and the grinding of air conditioners snugged into the window bottoms contributed little more than noise to the atmosphere of the place. But the computer worked, and the internet gave me what I was looking for.

The article was written in the formal language of the late 19th century, and it looked sideways at the sex and gore that would have splashed all over the page today, but both were there. Dusha Chuchonnyhoof had been convicted of a double murder, the victims the 23-year-old Lischen March, and her fiancé, 25-year-old Michael Miller.

The accused murderer had been found covered in blood, and clutching an iron key. There were innuendos, that Chuchonnyhoof had an unhealthy obsession with the young lovers before their deaths. The bodies of March and Miller were never discovered.

Nor was the door, opened by Chuchonnyhoof's key, though that was less of a priority.

It was the lack of corpses that saved Chuchonnyhoof from execution. The families of the engaged couple, March's family in particular, had begged and pleaded for the location of the bodies, but he'd maintained that he hadn't killed them.

The article made note that, after the trial, the jurors had all commented on the peculiar odor that surrounded Chuchonnyhoof. "Like burning iron," one said.

"Like the Devil himself."

I skimmed through a series of other articles that gave the same basic information, and then a few more mentions of the name, usually in articles about the legality of the death penalty on Oregon. His sentence had first been death by hanging, but the death penalty had been voted out of law in Oregon between 1914 and 1920. Chuchonnyhoof's sentence had then been commuted to "two lifetimes and a day," urged by March's family, who'd still hoped he would disclose the location of her body. The death penalty was voted back into legality, and in the late 1950s, he became a volunteer for execution by gas chamber. There was no information on him after that, but I couldn't tell whether it was that he'd faded from public interest—it had been years since his crime—or that the records were simply unavailable. I could find no death records, no obituary. I clicked a mention of Salem and the late 19th century, in some mid-1980s prison guard's memoir, intrigued momentarily, only to see that it was a tabloid story. *"I Guarded Deathless Prisoner," Says Guard.* Fittingly, a dead link. What was I doing? Tabloid news, and fake headlines.

I searched for Olivia Weyland. That gave me almost no information, other than the notice of her marriage into the Weyland family, and then her obituary in the local paper, confirming what I already knew from the circumstances of my possession of the house: the Weyland family was gone. They had died out, both by blood and by marriage, when Olivia did.

I raised my fingers from the keyboard, and then set them down again. One more search. "Rowan Mays."

Row.

My son.

A sob barked from my throat, and I smashed my hands against the keyboard, blanking the screen before I could read the things I knew were true. All the way fucking gone, Malcolm, I reminded myself, and every newspaper account, disagreeing on other things, would agree on that. He was dead.

"Sir? Can I help you?" A young woman in a floral sundress and worn cowboy boots stood next to me. "The computers can sometimes be frustrating. I'd be happy to help you put together your search."

"No." I sucked in a breath, and screwed my fists into my eyes. "No, thank you. Unhappy memory. I'm done now. I'll be fine."

"A glass of water, then? Those air conditioners aren't worth more than a promise." Her voice was cool in the heat, and her perfume like the heart of a forest. Had this been a different life, those things might have mattered. Even so, they were enough to remind me that this wasn't a different life. No one was coming back.

"I really am fine. I didn't mean to disturb you."

She smiled, and I almost smiled back.

"You didn't at all. I'm just here to help people. It's the end of the sentence, you know."

"What? What did you say?" I looked at her, shaken.

"It's the end of the summer, you know, later than it should be. October acting like August out there. Heat could kill you. Come back here if you need to cool off."

She smiled at me again, and tossed her long braid over her shoulder. I fled the library and everything in it.

I walked to the hardware store. The building looked like it might have grown up out of the ground, but inside, everything shone. Iron nails and pale, clean-smelling lengths of cut wood. Oil, and the chemical burn of paint. There was popcorn, hot and dripping with butter, in a machine just inside the door.

"Help yourself to a bag while you look around." The man who spoke had a lion's mane of white hair, and a sun-lined face. He wore jeans that looked like he worked in them, and a red t-shirt with the name of the hardware store—"Ralph's"—in curving script.

I lingered in the store while I ate the popcorn, looking at trim, tiles and plumbing fixtures, thinking of where I might put them in the house, once I could afford them. When I finished, I walked with my gallon of white latex paint back to the front of the store.

"That won't cover much, you know," said the man.

"I don't need much," I said. "Just one room, for now, where the graffiti's the worst."

"You must be the one who's moved into the Weyland place."

My throat clenched. I'd come here to get away from people, not to tell them where I was. "I am."

He looked at me, considering. "You planning on fixing it up?"

"As much as I can."

"Wait here, then. I've got something for you."

I thought about setting my money on the counter, taking the paint and leaving. I was certain I didn't want whatever it was he had. But I needed the change.

"Found it!" He was holding a manila envelope, faded with age. "It's been tucked away back there for a while, but I dug it out when I heard there was going to be a new owner. Glad to see you're doing something with the place. Come back when you're ready to start the real work, and I'll give you a deal on what you need."

Stamped across the back of the envelope, in red ink, was the word, "*PAID*." I felt an uneasy twinge, seeing it. Someone had stamped those letters from Chuchonnyhoof "Approved." Did a warden stamp them? Someone working at the prison, reading and sorting mail? That meant that in Salem, someone would know about those letters.

My fingers left smears on the envelope, sweat and popcorn grease, as I sat in the sweltering oven of my car to open it. Inside: two keys. Iron. Old-fashioned, and each clearly made to open a different door.

I reached up to the place in the ceiling where the letter had been. Nothing. Nothing under the seats, or between the cushions, or in the glove box. I put the lock and keys back into the envelope, and drove home.

7.

There were more letters on the floor when I got there. I stacked them up, and set them on the end table inside the door, weighing them down with the envelope from Ralph's.

Behind me, the mail flap clicked. Smiling up at me, again, from the floor, the picture of not-Row.

Do as I tell you, and he will be returned. You have the pieces. Instructions will follow.

"God damn it!" I yelled, and kicked the end table over. *Approved.* Who approved this? It was harassment, stalking, something. Letters fluttered through the air, and the envelope slid to the ground with a heavy thunk. I shoved a hand through my hair and stared at the mess, feeling stupid. "God damn it."

I took the can of paint upstairs. Painting over the graffiti might not be his plan for the day, but it was mine. As I painted, I made my mind as white as the wall. I covered over the red door, and along with it, I covered thoughts of other doors, with bodies behind them, thoughts of doors through which letters came unceasingly, doors through which my son would never walk, no matter what some impossible monster promised.

I painted, pushing the roller over the walls until they were clean, white and blank. When I was finished, I felt like I was the only one wearing my skin for the first time that day.

I washed, and went downstairs, looking for food. There was a cold supper in the refrigerator—a roast chicken, potatoes, green beans. An apple pie. Another bottle of wine. Even if the rest was wrong, the ghosts were kind. I ate and drank until I was full and drowsy.

There was a letter on my pillow upstairs.

Twenty-second October

My Dear Malcolm,

The end of the sentence is almost upon me. It is close enough that I allow myself to imagine—to imagine the sound of birdsong, the warmth of the sun on my skin, the taste of the wine I bottled, now more than one hundred years ago.

The End of the Sentence

I thought of the wine I'd drunk with my supper, and my stomach twisted.

> *I will return to you in ten days time.*
>
> *Forgive my vulgarity, Malcolm, but with the time so close upon us, I must speak more plainly than is my wont. The house, and its denizens, are bound to me, as I am bound to them. This binding must be made literal. I require shoes, and you must be the one to make them.*
>
> *Do not think you can avoid this duty, Malcolm. There are, as you know, consequences for a man who abdicates his responsibility.*
>
> *You have already been given the key. Find the door, and open it. Things will be clear once you do. Nearly everything that you require will be there.*
>
> *I look forward to that time when we may, like civilized men, discuss your remuneration. I keep my promises, Malcolm. I pay my debts.*
>
> *I am, imminently, yours.*
>
> *Dusha.*

8.

Ten days time. I felt alone, and not just alone. Afraid. What was being asked of me? I had to find out, ask someone, *tell* someone. I had to call the prison.

In the kitchen, I heard water running, dishes clattering against each other. Someone was humming, the faintest hum. A song, but I couldn't catch it. The sound made me want to cry, remembering my life in the world I'd left behind. Row being bathed in the kitchen sink. Then him in my arms in his towel, his little head against my chest. I was breathing too fast. Every time he was offered back to me, I believed it, and then I had to remember he was gone.

Fake. But what if it wasn't? Those stamps. *Approved.* Someone would know. I'd find someone who knew what he was. I felt drunk. I pictured my house, standing out here in the dead center of nowhere, no neighbors, no fence. I didn't have a gun. Nothing to protect myself, protect my house. What was being asked of me? Make shoes? Keys and bindings. Iron and doors? I didn't understand.

I had to call the prison. I was resolved, but as far as I could see, there weren't even any phone lines out here. Maybe they'd been taken away by whatever rural phone company there was, after the house next door caught fire. I didn't have a cell phone anymore. I'd dropped it in a trashcan somewhere in the Midwest, when the Greyhound pulled over to let lost souls stretch. Now I regretted it.

I drove into Ione again, late at night. Moon up, yellow and thin as a toenail clipping. My granddad had been a captain working in the Gulf of Mexico, but early in his career, he'd been second mate on a Norwegian freighter. I thought about a story he'd told me once, about a ship made of the nail clippings of the dead. I heard him again like I was six years old, sitting with him on his porch in New Orleans.

"Naglfar, they call it," said my granddad. "The nail-ship. At the end of the world, Naglfar comes loose from its mooring. You have to trim the fingernails of the dead, boy, or they go to build that ship. You don't want to leave a dead man with his fingernails long."

I saw my granddad's white beard, his dark skin, and his glittering eyes. He stretched his fingernails out to show me. Trimmed to the rind. He looked at my face, and then laughed.

"Your gran told me not to tell you those stories anymore, or you'll wet the bed, won't you?"

"Will not," I said. But I did, later that night, imagining the nail ship making its way through some terrible ocean, an anchor chain made of toenails, and a hull made of fingernails torn from their beds. I had nightmares about Naglfar for years. Now I was having waking nightmares about iron growing out of bones and I couldn't make sense of them. I imagined nails, iron nails. I'd read a story years before about a woman who grew fingernails instead of hair, and I imagined that for a drunken moment, a miserable creature covered in hard, sharp scales.

On the steering wheel, I looked at my own fingernails. For the first time in years I'd let them grow beyond their edges. What kind of fool thought he wasn't five minutes from dying? I shook my head. I was losing it.

Some old story, all of this. I was here, in Oregon, in October, working in heat hot enough to bake my brain. I didn't think I needed to go to a hospital, but then I wondered if maybe I did. I hadn't gone after what had happened at home. I couldn't imagine going to a hospital when it wasn't me who was injured, but my mother had tried to get me to go. "If you don't sleep, you die," she'd insisted, not realizing that dying was what I wanted.

Above me, there were shooting stars, and below me there were rabbits on the highway, white shapes moving across the black, discs of brightness that looked like floating Christmas lights, and then resolved into eyes. I swerved to keep from hitting them.

I drove past the grain elevators and the little cemetery, its stones yellow under the moon. None of my thoughts were good. Who was buried there? Was there a plot of earth waiting for a madman and a murderer?

Whatever he was, whoever he was, Dusha had given me ten days. I felt the unwilling tug of a kid forced onto a team for dodge-ball, standing on a gymnasium floor, the red rubber ball in my hands, a fast dodger, but a bad thrower. I'd always been a coward. Running from someone throwing me what I deserved. Eventually, I'd turn my back and it would hit, whatever was coming.

I needed to call the prison. I wanted to be punished, but it wouldn't fix what I'd done. They'd judged me not guilty, and in that moment I knew the gap between law and truth.

I felt guilty.

There were days I wanted to volunteer for execution myself. That picture of Row. In the picture, I saw my wife's face. He had her eyes. He had my mouth. Who knew what else he'd have had, had he lived? My bad judgment? Her anger?

I felt the jig of rocks under my wheels, and turned the car back into the road. Not sober. I drove to the diner.

Night, and lights glowing out over the dark high desert. It was full, and I wasn't expecting that, the windows showing me the population of Ione. There was Ralph from the hardware store, and the girl from the library, sitting at the counter on red vinyl stools that had seen better days. I stumbled out of my car and into the dark lot.

I had a sudden vision of the face of Dusha Chuchonnyhoof, looking up at me from under thick black eyebrows, but I didn't have any idea what Dusha looked like. I could only see his smile. It was a smile of certainty, that I would do what he wanted, that I was weak.

What was I doing? Trying to report someone already imprisoned? The letters were *Approved*, ruled safe.

There are, as you know, consequences for a man who abdicates his responsibility.

I hadn't slept in too many months, was all. Paint fumes and heatstroke too. I looked into the diner. It looked safe in there. Black coffee. A pot to myself, at the counter. Maybe I hadn't really been eating, either, but just imagining the meals served by ghosts. Maybe I was starving. I'd walk into the diner and start over. It was the American way. I could be allowed to erase my history. People did it all the time. Through the windows, I watched a woman pushing her plate away, a waitress silent movie-ing her hands in the air. I stood in the dark, longing for everything inside. I wanted them to see me, to make sure that I could be seen.

I realized suddenly that I didn't know what had happened to the people next door, my neighbors, the burnt-out rectangle. I didn't know if they'd lived or died or run off into the dark. I didn't know if they were in prison with Dusha.

I made it almost to the door, but there was a sound I couldn't place. I realized it was the hissing of the lights. I looked up at the diner sign.

LISCHEN'S DINER it said, blinking on and off. Then it didn't say that anymore, but something else entirely.

The letters blinked out completely one by one, until they read only HER. As they did, the girl from the library walked beneath them, unbraiding her hair. She turned her head, looked out the window, and saw me. She smiled. She waved her hand. She called me in.

HER.

The lights were red and blazing and I stared at them as she beckoned. The remaining letters of Lischen's Diner blinked back on, as though they hadn't been off. I walked to the diner door, and opened it, slowly. I hadn't been this drunk in a long time, and I hadn't even realized it was happening.

The guy from the hardware store turned around.

"Hey, there, fella," he said, and the way he said it was so friendly, I almost cried out in pain. "Have you tried the keys yet? They've been there years. Might be for locks you got, might not. The people who lived there were strange ones. You're not from that family, are you, boy?"

My knees buckled.

"I need to use the phone," I said. "I don't have one where I live."

The girl from the library was already on her feet.

"Are you okay? You don't look okay," she said. "How about some coffee?"

"He's the new guy," said Ralph. I swayed, catching myself on the back of a booth. The girl had a mug in her hand, and she was coming to me, concerned.

HER, the lights had said. Her.

"I'm Lischen," she said, and my guts slid sideways like a glass door.

"How is that?" I managed.

"How's what?" she said. "Lischen March. I know, it's a funny name, but it's in my family."

"You know you're—"

She smiled at me.

"Drink that coffee. This is my place," she said. "Well, it's my mom's place, anyway, and before that my grandma's. I know you. I work at the library. You went running out like dogs were after you. You're Malcolm, who bought the Weyland place. You're the talk of the town. Drink the coffee. We know what drunk looks like."

That perfume was still on her, a sweet, familiar forest smell, and her face was sweet too, and tender, sunburnt cheeks and hair bent from the braid she'd taken out. She was still wearing the same dress, flowers twining up from the hem to wrap around her. Maybe in her late twenties, not the teenager I'd first taken her for. I felt the ghost of the ring I'd had on my finger, and I pushed past her.

"I need to use the phone," I said. "It's urgent."

The guy behind the counter pushed an old phone at me. Rotary. I listened to the dial tone. I was real. There were people outside this town.

I caught myself dialing my old number. No. I put the receiver down again, with effort.

"I need a phone book."

He had one. Once I had it in my hands, I realized I had no idea what I was doing. This phone book wasn't for Salem. Salem was 200 miles away. I decided to try to trust them.

"I need to call the prison. The Oregon State Penitentiary, I think?"

They looked at me, all these innocent people in this innocent town. None of them knew anything about what was happening to me. I got off the stool, exhausted. This had been a mistake. Ten days allotted to me by a madman. It wasn't real.

Ralph sighed, and put his cup down on the counter.

"So you're looking for Ironhide," he said.

9.

I collapsed to the ground in a clattering heap of red-glitter vinyl and silver chrome diner stools. Shock, exhaustion, drunkenness, and there I was, crumbled on the floor, no legs left to stand on.

"Come on, now, fella. Up you come." Ralph picked up the stools, then tucked his hands under my arms and pulled me up as well. "Malcolm. Have a seat now, Malcolm."

He heaved me onto one of the stools, and Lischen set a slice of grasshopper pie in front of me. "It's on the house—a welcome to town," she said.

My brain was a page full of crossed-out writing.

"Ironhide," Ralph said. "No need to call the prison to find out anything about him. Eat up now. Everyone around here knows the story. Not the kind of thing we'd forget, even if Lischen weren't named for her great-aunt, God rest her soul."

"Why do you call him Ironhide?" I asked.

"Well, you can hardly expect a person to spit out his mouthful of a name every time, now can you? And besides, he had that condition. Give me a slice of that pie, too, Lischen."

She smiled as she slid the plate over to him, and the bracelet she wore glinted in the light from the fluorescents overhead. Normal things. I could barely hold myself still in my seat. Better to be back on the floor, where the world might stop tilting. They were acting as if Dusha Chuchonnyhoof was nothing.

"Exactly," Ralph said.

"What?"

"That name you just said. Dusha whatever it was." Ralph took a bite of his pie.

I hadn't realized I had spoken.

"Condition?" I asked.

"Something to do with too much iron in his blood. Made him rust from the inside. And he smelled like iron, stank of it, if you got too close to him. Some said that's what turned him into the monster he was, but I believe he was a monster already, to do what he did." Ralph shook his head, his great mane of hair haloing out with the motion.

"Did it make him immortal, too?" I took a small bite of the pie, and then another, larger one.

"Good, isn't it?" Ralph asked. "Lischen bakes them. And no. He wasn't immortal. Ironhide is good and dead. Has been for years. They executed him, way back when."

He looked at me, his eyebrow up.

"But" *I've been receiving* "there are letters" *from him* "from the prison" *saying he's returning* "to tell me his sentence is almost over." In my head, the words I could not spit out echoed.

"That was the condition of the commutation of the sentence," Lischen said, her voice so quiet I could hear the sign outside crackle and spark. "When he wouldn't tell the location of the bodies. My family never gave up hope he would, that confronting his own illness and death might cause compassion in him, and so we asked that he not be put to death. But we also wanted justice. So unless he confessed, and told where to find them, his body would remain in the prison, in its cell, for two lifetimes and a day."

I looked up at her. "Why the extra day?"

She startled, then relaxed. "A day to punish him for any other sin, I guess. Maybe they thought he'd done more than they knew."

"The letters are just to tell you it's almost time to come and get the remains. Condition of buying the Weyland house, I expect," said Ralph, his fork screeing across his empty plate.

But the letters are from him. "But why would the prison expect the Weyland family to take responsibility for his body?"

"The family worked for him, way back. Blacksmiths. Ironhide was the one who bought the place for them, that and all the land around it. Olivia, the lady who owned the house before you, sold off some of the land when things went hard for her," said Ralph. "But check your papers. Some of it at least should still be yours.

"I'm sure the Board of Corrections just wants some money to bury the bastard with. No one actually expects you to sling a body in your trunk and drive off."

Lischen cleared my empty plate. "Can I get you anything more?"

"No, thank you. You've been very kind."

"Better to take care of someone." She began wiping down the counter. The diner had emptied itself of all but the three of us.

"It's late. I should be going."

"Are you going to be able to get yourself back safe, now? It's no bother for me to run you out there," Ralph said.

"I'm better, thanks."

He looked at me, then nodded. "You'll feel better still once you get that place cleared out. I can come out to help, you need it."

"Ralph, it's late to be drumming up business. Let the poor man get home." Lischen smiled at me. "Drive safe, now."

I sat in the car for a minute, head tipped back against the cracked leather of the seat, waiting for the spinning that had nothing to do with drink to stop. The sign blinked, and across my windshield, again, in letters of bleeding red, *HER*.

I rolled down all the windows to let the night into the car as I drove home.

I wanted to believe those good, logical explanations. It was easier to think there was some hidden clause in the papers I'd signed, something that said I needed to pay for a murderer's burial, than to think that the pages and pages of letters littering my hallway were written by that same iron-skinned murderer. Better to think that, even if it meant realizing that my grip on sanity was less than I'd thought after Row's death.

The car thumped and skidded, wheels off the shoulder and into the dirt. I wrenched the steering wheel back to true. A dead rabbit, twisted and broken, on the side of the road.

(My child, my boy, twisted and broken.)

I tightened my grip on the steering wheel, dead man's nails biting in, and pushed those wishes and wants out of my head until I turned into my driveway.

I wanted to believe Lischen and Ralph, but want and truth didn't sleep well in the same bed together.

10.

I woke to find my sheets twisted like a noose around my neck. The room smelled stale and sour, last night's alcohol still seeping from my pores. My head throbbed like a rotted tooth.

I went into the bathroom, opened the mirrored medicine cabinet, and found what I was looking for on the rusted white shelves. Clippers, to trim my nails.

In the kitchen, there was bacon, done until crisp, two eggs over hard, and toast, with a heavy glass jar of strawberry preserves next to it. There was also coffee, in a blue enamelware pot I hadn't known I had. Leaning against the coffeepot was a letter.

Twenty-third October

My dear Malcolm,

I am not dead, though it bothers me not that others think me so. It is easier, in this fashion, for me to go about my business unhindered. Well. Unhindered except for the temporary inconvenience of my imprisonment, but that is about to change.

Nine days more, Malcolm, and then my shoes, my shoes. There are things which must be done in advance of my arrival, the hour of which draws ever nearer.

You have been given the key, Malcolm. Open the door.

If I could speak more plainly to you I would. I have no great love for unnecessary mysteries, particularly between friends. We are friends, are we not? The house cares for you, and it would not, if you were my enemy. But I too am bound by the bargains that were struck when I was imprisoned, and while this mystery is a solvable one, it must be you who plucks out the heart of it.

Time is sliding through the glass. Find the door and find your answers.

Yours,

Dusha.

Better, I thought, to know what it was that he wanted, than to wait until the clock ticked down to disaster. I went back to my room, and collected the keys.

"I need," I said to the ghosts, the house, the hauntings, "the door."

There was a muffled, heavy sound. Something large moving. A scrape, and a shriek of metal long unused and now forced into movement. A piece of paper fluttered through the air to land in the center of my bed.

Down. I swallowed.

The front hallway was as it had been, letters stacked on the end table, and gathered in the willow-branch and reed basket. A breeze came through the hallway, rustling the piles of paper. The kitchen door was open.

A huge pile of brush had been pulled away from the side of the house, exposing a metal storm door, ringed with the thorned canes of some sort of bush. The door stood open. I could see a set of stairs leading down, and I could not see where they ended.

Better to know.

The crumpled shells of dead insects crunched beneath my feet. Cobwebs clung to my head and hands, and I could hear the skitterings of small animals. There was another scratching, more deliberate and regular, behind me. I turned.

Take care.

I kept walking down. There were oil lamps on the walls that flared and smoked into life just enough ahead of my steps that the path was illuminated for me. The keys in my pocket clanked against each other as I walked.

And then, the door.

I steeled myself. The articles I'd read in the library had not said how extensive the search for the bodies of Lischen March (a smile, a floral dress, and a scent like sunshine and cedar and *no, you idiot, not her*) and Michael Miller had been.

It was the second key that worked. The lock turned, and the door, for all its weight, opened smoothly on its hinges. The air smelled of iron.

It was a large room, high-ceilinged enough to nearly counteract the press of the earth on all sides. And it was clear that I'd been walking out from the house under the earth, because there was a large oven, a furnace, with a chimney stretching up from it, and there was no chimney in my house.

There were no skeletons, no bodies. But in the center of the room was an anvil, marked with the same C&W that had been on the brand. There was a sledgehammer too, angled beside it as though it had been dropped. Rusted, everything, a rime on the hammer, and on the wooden handle the marks of a small hand's grip. The movement of my feet stirred up red dust. *Dried blood on my hands and under my nails and.* No. Then, not now.

I put my hands in my pockets, trying to make sure I left no prints on anything, and again, I didn't know why.

I wasn't a criminal. I was just a man in the dark, on his land, looking over the vault beneath it. I thought about the smoke I'd seen days before, in the burned out rectangle where the meth house had been. The chimney. The forge. The smoke. Nothing on fire, but maybe—

A breeze came through the chimney, a sudden whistling, and a bird flew out and into the room, fast and frantic, the panicked flapping of wings. My heart lurched, but it wasn't coming for me.

I looked up, and in looking up saw what was waiting. The instructions? The nest was a twiggy mass beneath one of the lamps mounted to the wall, and there were eggs in it. Eggs and an envelope, written not on the prison form, but the old stationery I'd seen once before.

Mrs. Paul Weyland. Olivia.

The letter was dated two years earlier. A shaking hand, pencil, lines crossed out throughout. I strained to make it out in the half-light.

11.

Dear Stranger,

I'll be dead by the time anyone finds this letter. I leave it for you, on the chance it helps. ~~Though I fear this can't be helped. There seems no remedy, not prayer, not sacrifi~~

By the time I came to this place, everyone who'd known me was dead. My dear Paul, who'd spent his life running from Ione ~~and his responsibility here.~~ *My parents and sister, who'd cautioned me against marrying him. I loved him. I did as I pleased. Now I bear the consequences, and if you are reading this, I've passed them to you. I am sorry for that. I tried.*

I was Olivia Jones, who married into the Weylands, and into this land. I wasn't young when

71

I came. Now I'm older than I ought to be. The house has kept me, feeding me, petting me. The doctor in town has died, and so has his son. Now I see his granddaughter, who thinks I'm a nice old lady.

I am not. I'm a woman who married into a monster. I am a woman who vowed herself into a debt, a woman who wore a white dress and a veil, and I said that I would accompany my husband where he went. I said I'd walk beside him. I did that, and when he died, I thought I'd die of sorrow, but I didn't. No one dies of sorrow.

Everyone I know is dead or in that prison in Salem, and that person, I met only once.

I inherited the thing they call Ironhide, who I know as Dusha Chuchonnyhoof. Maybe you'll inherit him also, as I did, unknowing. If so, you are as cursed as I am. I left my duties too long, and now, I'm not strong enough to do them. I could scarcely make my way down into this dark, and light the forge. I knew it was here all these years. How could I ignore it, you'll ask? I did. Perhaps you will try to ignore it too.

I went to church of a Sunday, and at night I prayed for deliverance. ~~Something from Hell, I thought, and now I don't know. Perhaps Dusha Chuchonnyhoof is from Heaven and Heaven is not what we thought.~~

I thought the house would help me, but those who live in the house—perhaps now I am one of them, serving you your dinner, filling your bath, laundering your shirts—cannot work down here. Ghosts and iron don't mix. He, though, mixed with the Weylands, and married them, or so he says. Someone of that family married him, once, long ago, and made him promises, just as I made promises to Paul.

I met him once, did I write that already? I met him. It was 1958.

"I have lost all hope, Olivia," he'd written. "You have no child, and I have no one left to give me what I need. I've volunteered for execution. Come and pray for me. I am a thing of metal and bones. My shoes are breaking and my feet blister, Olivia."

He sent me an invitation. The prison stamped it "Approved." I put on my Sunday hat, and took the bus to Salem. He'd written me thousands of letters by then. I was a Christian woman. I was lonely here in this strange house, in this strange place, and I had grown fond of him. Devils tempt, and men too.

I thought I might love him, though I knew love could not help him. Love was not what he wanted. Not from me.

By then, the executions were done by gas chamber, and no longer by hanging. When I was a girl in

Nevada, a hanging was called a necktie social, and the town would dress in their best to attend, but here, they'd changed it to the gas chamber after too many bad deaths.

I went to Dusha Chuchonnyhoof's execution.

A tiny room with metal walls, a black leather and wood chair, a window to the hallway where we all stood. He was inside the chamber for two hours, alive under the hood, as the gas poured into the room. At last, they walked him out, and I was there. He hobbled on stiff legs, and I heard the thin clack of his shoes. They'd taken off the hood.

He smiled at me then. Have you seen him yet? Have you met him? The end of the sentence approaches, he's told me, for years now. Perhaps you have.

He's a small man. His hair is short and dull, the color of iron, and his mouth is always smiling. His skin is rust red. His eyes are blue, and they will upset you. He knew me instantly.

"Olivia," he said. "My dear, I seem to live for you."

They tried to hang Dusha Chuchonnyhoof as well, though I doubt you'll find record of it. Dusha Chuchonnyhoof didn't hang. Later, after I left the prison, I'm told they tried to shoot him, all the men behind a screen, their rifles through it, and him, standing there in his hood, but the bullets made no difference to his body.

The End of the Sentence

As I write this letter, Dusha Chuchonnyhoof lives. Two lifetimes and a day he will remain there, and then he will come home unbound. Unbound, stranger. I don't know what that means, but I have nightmares that don't fade with the sunrise. I thought I could do what he asked. I lit the fires. I brought the hand. But there is not enough of me left, and though I could throw myself into the fire, it wants a blacksmith and another, two others. You must give it two more, or it will never be done. One is not enough for this. ~~What could I do here, all alone? Who could help me? I tried but the bad people in the house next door couldn't give me what I needed, stranger, and they were dead of their poison (and maybe it was not their poison that killed them. Maybe it was mine. I have a cabinet full of pills here, and what addict wouldn't want a gift?) before I tried, but the bargain requires the living and the loving. So I~~

~~I lit a fire to hide my mistakes.~~

I couldn't perform the anvil marriage alone. Paul is dead. He died and was buried, as any Christian man should be. I am buried if you read this. Who will mourn me but Dusha Chuchonnyhoof?

You'll find part of me here, on the horn. I tried. It was all I could do, and it wasn't enough. The task needs the living.

*I wish you the grace of the Lord, whoever you are.
I go up from here to die, I think. I hope I go to die.*

Olivia Jones Weyland

I looked around the room, my throat closing, but there was no one here. Just me, in the dark, with the oil lamps and the anvil. I knelt to examine the piece of metal that still hung looped over the pointed end. The *horn*, some memory dredged up. The *horn*, the *shoulder*, the *foot*, the *body*, the *face*, the *waist*, the *heel*. Metalshop. High school. Flunking out of everything but the blaster class, the anvil like a woman's body before me, and my heart the red hot metal waiting to be shaped.

It was a horseshoe, the thing hanging from the horn. My hands stretched out, wanting to take its hand in mine.

Its hand? No. Yes. The horseshoe was made of iron fingers, connected end to end, a thumb and an index finger stretching into the arc, another pair of fingers attached to the tips of the first. It wasn't symmetrical. The nails were long and feminine. (I shuddered at the length, Naglfar's materials.) Perfect replicas. The level of detail, down to the fingerprints, etched in perfect hairline scratches. All this, meant to be nailed to a hoof, and never seen by anyone but the farrier.

Farrier? The word surfaced in my brain like something fished up from the bottom of a lake. One of the fingers wore a wedding ring, an old-fashioned solitaire, but the diamond and gold were iron too.

The horseshoe clattered on the floor. I'd been imagining cobbling, tanning hide, working the leather, using small nails to make a pair of shoes, but this was something else. There were no horses here, not that I'd seen, though this was horse country.

There were things I could make of iron, maybe, dim memories of high school. A nail. If I was lucky, a basic horseshoe, for a normal horse. The bend was tricky, pounding the metal into the proper shape to fit a hoof. Nothing like what lay at my feet, a macabre wonder of craftsmanship. Craftswomanship? Had Olivia Weyland somehow made that shoe?

You'll find part of me here.... Perfect replicas of fingers, down even to perfect fingerprints.

Had Olivia Weyland somehow become that shoe?

Oil lamps and an anvil, rust on everything in the room. No footprints, but the mark of a hand, small. A great furnace, waiting for a fire.

Smoke, rising above the burned-out square of earth.

I knelt to check the hearth, and make sure it was cool. The thought of leaving a fire still burning beneath my land was a bad one. The forge was cold, but as my fingers sifted through the ashes, one of the bricks of the hearth shifted as well. There, beneath it, I found the instructions Dusha Chuchonnyhoof had promised.

They were written on parchment, rather than paper. At least, I hoped that the skin I held had once been that of an animal. The lines were in a hand I did not know, pointed and full of flourishes.

A Method for the Binding of the Goblin Chuchonnyhoof

> *Necessary to complete the binding are the hands of two who are themselves bound by vow, bound by love and bound with their hands atop the anvil. Only two such hands made into shoes will hold the Goblin bound in its proper form, so that it may walk among others in the shape of a man.*

Images unfolded in my mind as I read. I saw this room, and two young people, their hands clasped together over the anvil, Lischen March, identical to her great-niece, and a man who must have been Michael Miller. I could not see his face, but she was weeping.

> *The blacksmith must also be bound, by vow and to the line Weyland. The binding of love is not here required, though it may strengthen that which is here done. It must be a blacksmith who stands at the forge, for the work of a whitesmith will strike false.*

The End of the Sentence

I saw just their hands, and the surface of the anvil, slick with blood. It seemed as though I could smell the heat of the forge and the blood too.

The shoes will be made of iron, for there is iron in the blood, and without both, the shape cannot be made to hold. The iron shoes must be quenched in the blood of those whose hands have been given, those hands made iron.

In my mind, the result of this ceremony, a set of horseshoes like the one that Olivia had left. Hands, perfect, twinned together, still faintly glowing from the heat, steam rising from them.

And when this is done, the shape of the Goblin shall be held in the form of man, and the souls shall be preserved, and what is lost will be returned, and made perfect.

There were the iron shoes, nailed to a pair of hooves, and there was a man matching the description Olivia's letter had given of Dusha Chuchonnyhoof, and there was Lischen March and Michael Miller, and they were whole and hale.

And there was my son, Rowan Mays, smiling.

And should the binding be prevented, or left incomplete, the shape shall be twisted, and the death shall be the death of iron.

And there was a monster, covered in blood, wailing, roaring, screaming. I could not say which.

Nine days.

12.

I woke that night from a deep and drunken sleep—the
house had provided comfort of its kind—to light streaming in from beneath the bedroom door. Soft footsteps,
Row up from a nightmare. I rolled over, hoping my wife
would tend him, but no. I stretched out an arm to touch
her shoulder and wake her, and felt a warmth where she'd
been, smelled a sweetness like dead leaves in the woods.
She must be up to get him already. Outside my bedroom
door, the hall was full of feet, running through the house.

I settled back into the bed, still half-sleeping, antic-
ipating her return. She'd come back, warm and silky as
a mountain lion, her smell of silver jewelry and cedar.
She'd nestle into the bed beside me, her belly against my
back, her thigh over mine, and her breath against my
neck, her teeth—

There was a sound like something peeling back, a scratching and an unsealing. I jolted up, my heart racing. No, that was a dream. The sound, the weight in the bed, the sharp teeth and—

I turned my head.

There was light pouring in from beneath the door. Not the bedroom door. The painted door in the wall. I'd left the key on the dresser, and now it protruded from the plaster.

I stopped breathing. I'd painted over the red rectangle, and the new latex was still there, but light was beginning to come through it, all around its edges. Somewhere I heard sobbing, faint and desolate.

Was I awake? The smell of silver and cedar, and that was real. The invisible door started to open, outward from the room, into nothing, the rectangle of white paint remaining, stretched across an emptiness.

As I watched, the paint moved, something pressing against it from behind. A female face began to appear, white and gleaming, lips and cheekbones, nose and eyelids, pushing toward me, into my room. I recognized it, or almost did. It was dark, but light poured out beneath the painted door, from somewhere I didn't want to see. Beside the first face, another began to coalesce. Strong brows, this one, a beard. A sharp nose.

I watched as their bodies pressed into the thin screen of paint separating us, and as they raised their left arms, I steeled myself, clutching the bedside lamp, for the moment they discovered they could claw through the barrier and into the room. They didn't move. Their arms ended in nothing. No hands. They stood, holding them up, as if to show me the absence. At last, slowly, they receded, as though they'd walked backward. The light faded. The key fell out of the lock that wasn't, and clacked on the floor, jolting me into a frenzy of shaking and shuddering.

I heard hoofbeats. A horse, somewhere, galloping away. Or something else in horseshoes.

The smell of coffee brewing. The house wasn't sleeping, and neither was I.

I looked at the pillow beside me and saw an indentation in it. A long black hair. Coarse, yet soft as raw silk. I coiled it up, into a knotted tangle.

I got out of bed, my feet freezing on the floor, though I could feel the strange October heat pressing on the house already. I picked up the key, and the photograph of Row, and went downstairs, the hair in my hand to be thrown outside as soon as I could.

On my kitchen table, I wasn't surprised to find the horseshoe, though I didn't remember picking it up. In my hallway, I wasn't surprised to find a new letter from Dusha Chuchonnyhoof.

In my hand, I wasn't surprised to find the sledge-hammer, heavy and perfectly weighted, the indentations in the handle sized to my grip. The end of the sentence was approaching, and there was work to be done. I had responsibilities.

I would find a person *(HER)* *(not her)* whose hands could be bound in an anvil marriage, and then I'd...

I'd turn the hands into horseshoes, blood and iron to bind to the feet of Dusha Chuchonnyhoof, someone else's hands to keep his feet from touching the earth. If I did it right—I hefted the sledgehammer—if I followed the instructions, somehow everything would be fine and Row would be alive and the end of the sentence was approaching and I had a duty and I—

My coffee cup clattered on the table, bringing me back to my senses.

Jesus.

What was I thinking? What the hell was I thinking? Phantom advisors, horrible nightmares, and I was here thinking of taking—no, call it what it is, *cutting off*— someone's hands?

Malcolm, Malcolm, you came here running from your past, and now you were thinking of doing something horrible to someone else? Because some creature instructed you to? Because you found a piece of paper telling you to commit a crime?

No. I sat down at the kitchen table (coffee, in front of me, steaming, comfort, refilled again to replace the cup I'd spilt) and wrote a letter on the brown paper sack from the hardware store.

The End of the Sentence

Chuchonnyhoof,

I didn't buy you with this land, and you don't own me as part of your claim. You promise me something that can't exist. I don't invite you into my life. It belongs to me, even if nothing else does. Don't look to me to do your work. Stay in prison, or go elsewhere, but you will not return here. The end of your sentence is nothing to me. I'm not your man. Someone put you in prison. If you come here, I'll put you back there.

Don't contact me again.

Malcolm Mays

I weighed it down with a rock, left it on the porch, and went back inside, slamming the door behind me. I wouldn't just sit here waiting for letters. I'd felt passive, here in this house, fed, clothed and bathed like a child, and now I'd responded, however insane it seemed.

I should mail the letter like a normal person, not put it out for the post to pick up. As far as I could tell, there was no post. Still, the deliveries were to my door, and so I'd send it that way, too. As though the birds and wind would deliver my letter to someone who didn't exist.

Ironhide, not a goblin but a murdering man, jailed a hundred and seventeen years ago. He would be a skeleton now, and I'd been summoned by the jail to give the money for the burial. It would be a potter's field for him. I wouldn't pay to have Ironhide come home, even in a box. What did I owe him? This land was cursed enough, or seemed to be. I wanted to grow things here, and sweep the dust out, and work my way back into living a life.

In my head, my wife said again the last things she'd said to me: "Get out of this house, Malcolm. You're not even a sorry excuse. You're nothing."

She slammed my hand in the door as she pushed me out.

"You say you love me," she yelled out the window. "But you don't love anyone but yourself. Poor Malcolm who accidentally killed his son. Poor Malcolm who accidentally broke his wife's heart. Poor Malcolm who accidentally deserves nothing he ever had. Get the hell away from me. Never come back here."

I thought again of Row, an avalanche of loss, and the promise this thing, this goblin (goblin?) had made to me. The return of my son.

That parchment hadn't come into the house. I looked frantically around the kitchen. No. It wasn't here.

Row, I thought, Row. These thoughts, the dreams, must only be my brain, trying to reorganize its contents. I thought of the stories I'd told my son before bed, the ship stories passed down from my grandfather. My granddad had been around the world, and collected things in ports, stories of goblins and haystacks, ships on roiling seas, the wolf Fenris, the Irish shifting creatures who tugged at hems and tore at skirts. He told them all like he was telling the truth. Row hadn't really liked those stories. He wanted stories about beautiful things instead, and now I didn't blame him. He wanted to watch princesses on the television. His mother, at his begging, bought him a crown and a dress, and he wore them. A little boy who insisted he was something other than the thing he seemed to be. That never went well in the world. I worried. But he was still so little.

The last thing Row said to me was "I'm a princess, Daddy."

And I thought, "There's no such thing as that happy ending."

I tucked him in, and went downstairs to fight with his mother, our traditional fight about money, lasting until we were both too tired to stop ourselves from saying the worst possible things.

I shut my eyes and rubbed my fists over them. A flash of satin. A cheap gilded crown with rhinestones all over it. Headlight, I thought. The kind of headlight you might not have bothered to get replaced, thinking you knew your way home on faith in the dark.

My coffee was full again. It was dawn, and I could see the sun rising out the windows.

I thought about iron shoes. Only sinners wore iron shoes.

The flap on the front door clicked open, but no letter fell through it. It set up a tremendous rattling, as if a tornado twisted on the other side of the door. The letters on the end table and in the woven basket flew into the air, and set up a whirlwind of their own, spinning and whiting out my vision.

"What the hell is going on?" I yelled. The letters dropped to the ground. The mail flap held still.

A knock on the door.

Lischen March stood on the dirt path, a plate covered by a red gingham cloth in her hands. "Good morning! I thought you might be feeling a little rough, so I brought breakfast. Well, they're popovers, so good anytime, really. Sorry it's so early, but I saw the light on."

The hot, eggy scent of the popovers curled into my doorway. People had brought food, when Row died. Casseroles in heavy dishes and containers of soup, frozen, "for later." They stop bringing the food when they realize the death is your fault. I felt nauseous.

I stepped back out of the doorway. "Thanks. Um. Come in."

The letters were stacked, neatly, in the woven basket, under the table, and mostly out of sight. The sledgehammer was nowhere to be seen. Lischen looked around.

"How bad was the place when you moved in?" she asked.

"About what you'd expect, I guess," I said. I poked my head into the refrigerator, looking for the pot of strawberry preserves, but the shelves were bare.

"I don't have much besides coffee to offer you," I said.

"Coffee'd be great," she said. "Ralph said there was all sorts of scary graffiti on the walls." She tilted her head and looked at me. "People always want to say stuff like that is done by Satanists, but I don't think there are too many devil worshippers hanging out in Ione." She laughed.

"It wasn't good," I said, "but it wasn't like that either. It's gone now. I painted over it."

"You should've shown me. I'm a librarian—I like interesting things."

Faces, pressing out from a wall. Handless arms reaching. No.

The light glinted against her left wrist as she reached for the mug. A cuff of two hands tightly linked together in shining white metal. "That's a pretty bracelet."

"Thank you. I do some metal working, as a hobby," she said, and smiled.

A forge and a furnace and a hand hanging over a horn. I felt a sudden flood of relief. Maybe she was the one the letter meant, not me at all, maybe this was HER—

"Like a blacksmith?" I asked.

"Why, do you have a horse out back that needs shoeing?" She laughed.

Nothing like a horse, but oh, yes. Shoes were required. "Wouldn't that be something if I did."

Lischen set the mug back down on the table, next to a letter from the prison. I felt an urge to tug it out of her way, but she put her hand on it before I could.

"Is this one of the ones you've been getting?" she asked.

"Yeah," I said, feeling exposed. A fraud, somehow. I suddenly thought I might have written them myself.

Approved, said the letter. Red ink. The same as always. The house said nothing, and nothing moved but the two of us.

She slit the envelope with her long fingernail, and unfolded the contents. I found I wasn't breathing.

"Yes," she said, nodding. "Like Ralph thought. They just want to know what you want them to do with his hide. Says this is the final notice."

I looked up. "His hide?"

"His body," she said. "Hide? What did you think I said?"

"Nothing."

"Okay," she said, and smiled. "It's weird out here, right? It's too far out for most people. Gets too dark at night and too bright in the day. I'm working at the library today. Short hours on Sunday, but come by anytime if there's something I can help you with. It can be hard, moving into a strange place, with all sorts of obligations that you weren't expecting."

I walked her back to the front door. "Thanks for stopping by. And the food. It was kind of you." I realized I had a question. "Olivia Weyland. Did you know her?"

"Of course," she replied. "She used to come into the library all the time. She knew a lot about the history of this area, got a correspondence degree from somewhere back East. It was sad what happened to her."

I wasn't sure I wanted to know. But no. That was a coward's way. That was the old Malcolm.

"What happened exactly? I thought—I figured she just died of old age or something." I had looked her up, at the library. What had I missed?

She looked steadily at me and my skin felt somehow both stroked and scraped. Her voice, maybe. The sweet roughness in it. Again, I wondered how old she was. In her thirties, I thought now, not twenties. My age, even. There were fine lines at the corner of her mouth, lines that suited her. Her fingernails were polished an iridescent pearl color. I wondered where she'd gotten the nail polish.

"Well, this is two years ago now, so that's maybe why no one told you," Lischen said. "It's pretty bad, too. Nobody wants to talk about it. The people next door. Thought they'd rob her, but something went wrong. I went to high school with a boy from that family. They were trouble since forever. Famous in these parts for it. The Millers were some of the people that settled Ione, and they'd been going down a long time." She shrugged. "They cut her hand off for her rings, the police said. I guess they couldn't get them off. She had arthritis."

"Her hand," I said. "I thought—"

"What'd you think? Yeah," Lischen said. "Her left hand. But then they all died too. There was an explosion and a fire over there. Well, you can see what happened. Scorched earth. The Millers are all gone now, and the Weylands too. My family's the only one from back then still here and prospering."

She laughed, and it rang out weirdly in the kitchen. We were talking about murder, about drugs, about an old woman's hand being cut off. I tried to reshuffle my mind, the things I thought I knew.

She patted the table.

"Don't worry. I wasn't laughing about Olivia Weyland and the Millers. I was laughing about prospering. Library full of old paper, and a diner full of pie, those are my family heirlooms. Come in and get dinner if you want to, later. Blackberry pie tonight. They're ripe to bursting. See these stains on my mouth? You've got some out back. Bring them by and I'll make you some jam. Got to put something on those popovers."

She grinned at me, and the grin was ridiculous, dizzy-making. She was right. Her lips were stained. I had to remind myself who I was, a man who'd fled his life, and for good reasons. I couldn't have anything like what that grin looked like. Happiness wasn't simple for me. I thought of my marriage. It was taking me too long to let her go, but that didn't mean it wasn't over. Once you run away, you can't go back.

"Maybe I'll see you later," I managed.

"Hope so," she said, and put her hand on my shoulder for a moment. I jerked back. It'd been a long time since anyone had touched me, and it felt wrong, until I remembered that this was what people did. They touched other people. It was normal.

"Sorry," I said, embarrassed.

"No need," she said. "Everybody comes from something. I figure you've got a history like anyone, don't you, Malcolm Mays? I have a history too."

I stood in the doorway and watched her hop into a faded red pickup truck, draping one arm out the window as she drove off. She hadn't just appeared here. Of course she hadn't, I reminded myself. The town was real. Lischen was real, not part of this house. I rubbed my shoulder, sore where she'd touched it, and watched the dust of her departure until she was all the way gone.

I looked down. My letter to Chuchonnyhoof was gone too.

There was silence in the house after she left. No breath, no singing, no sounds of dishes in the sink being washed. Maybe the house didn't like visitors.

Maybe the letter had changed things.

I felt at peace for a moment, standing outside the house, even having heard the sad story of Olivia. The sun was out, and there was a breeze and my house was silent. Maybe I wasn't going to live this way forever. I'd cleared the brush away from my old life, and resisted temptations. I could stay here. I felt, however insanely, however strangely, safe.

The sky was clear and blue. A haze of faint black smoke curled up from the scorched property, reminding me of what had been here. If I was going to clean the house of hazards, I'd need to make sure that chimney was clear.

The October sun hit me like a wall, but the patches of violets and mint, cool and green, had grown even further, as if they'd been planted in a different season. I walked five steps before yellow grass crackled beneath my feet. Behind the house were the blackberries she'd said were there, bushes by the door, leafed now and heavy with fruit, twisting up outside the kitchen windows, though I remembered bare vines. I put a berry in my mouth. Sour and sweet at once, the thorns on the vines scratching me as I reached for the berries, heavier than they looked, laden with black juice.

In the eastern corner of the scorched section, I found the hole in the ground, smoke drifting up from it. The earth felt hot. I tried again to realign what I'd thought the night before, with what Lischen had just told me. Ironhide was dead. Olivia Weyland was dead too, and in sad circumstances. The forge was below me, yes, but that meant nothing. This was a family of blacksmiths. It had said it in the newspapers, even. Something else too, some trigger to my memory, and I finally remembered. The Millers. Michael Miller was the other victim of Dusha Chuchonnyhoof.

I went to high school with a boy from that family. They'd been going down a long time.

Of course she had, though. This was a tiny town. Everyone knew everyone, except me. I knew the house, but I didn't know who the ghosts were, feeding me, bathing me, dressing me. It occurred to me that I might miss them if they were gone. Lischen's presence had been strange, a real person joining me in my house, even as I'd gotten accustomed to the kindness of invisible people.

The iron scent was strong here, strong enough to cover over the carbonized dirt, to almost obscure the sour chemical tang that lingered in the air from the poison that had been made here. I cleared the soot, chunks of wood and leaves from the top of the chimney, pushed the earth away from metal that was warm to the touch. The wind picked up, moving the heat through the air, making the sweat dry sticky and salt on my skin.

Something shone in the dirt, and I knelt, scrabbling for the shine.

A hand grabbed mine.

I reeled back from the dirt, and it came with me, bones clutching at my fingers. It caught and ripped at my skin. I could not shake it loose.

Not a hand. A horseshoe. Like the one Olivia had left on the anvil's horn, but unlike as well. Clumsy, half-formed. Fingers that were more like claws, with rough edges. This was someone's hand, iron, left here to rust. I stood, staring at it, wanting to fall down. Here it was. She'd told me.

I thought of how Olivia Weyland had prayed for me. I'd go and pray for her. And Row. All my wrongs. All my rights, in one little body.

I picked up the awful horseshoe and wrapped it in my shirt. I went inside and put the other horseshoe—there it was, kicked beneath the table—into a cloth napkin. Shrouded, my brain told me.

I wasn't a churchgoing man. I was someone who wished he could muster the hope it would take to believe in anything. But it was Sunday.

13.

I walked into town. The car wouldn't run for me. My hands were full of scraps of metal, wrapped in cloth. I walked, and as I walked, I talked to myself. I wrote myself a letter, as though someone loved me enough to send me comfort. My faults were my own, but people had loved me despite them.

Dear Malcolm,

You'll never be forgiven, but you'll forget the pain a little. Your son will not be returned to you, but you will keep living.

You will not forgive yourself, but it isn't necessary to forgive yourself. Mistakes are made, and you live with them. No one ever died of sorrow, Malcolm.

I realized I was quoting Olivia Weyland, even in my head.

I passed the cemetery, this sad little stand of white stones like tree stumps. I hopped a fence, thinking to visit Olivia's grave, and looked for the original Lischen March, and for Michael Miller, but they were nowhere to be seen. Someone still waiting for a prison letter that never came, a letter saying where to find the bodies. I found Weylands and Marchs all over, though, this town seemingly filled with them. A small section of Millers, off to the side, all in a row, grass dead atop them, just as the grass was dead beneath them on my land.

There was a grave set off to the side of the rest, a simple monument, with a small hand etched in lines of silver at the top of it. The only writing, "My son."

I brushed at my prickling eyes, and nearly fell over a small metal marker, stabbed into the earth as though the person below it was a row of seeds planted for the harvest.

Olivia Jones Weyland, it said. I looked at the marker more closely. There was something written on the metal, after her last name, etched in with a sharp tool, not colored as the rest of the letters were.

Olivia Jones Weyland Chuchonnyhoof

And below it, the mark I'd seen on the brand. The C tangled with the W.

I stood up, panting. Graffiti, someone messing with the graves. More Chuchonnyhoof's there, and there, on some of the other stones, scratched into stone, scribbled on in pencil.

On the road beside the cemetery, a beige truck idled, a horsetrailer attached to the back of it. Ralph leaned out the window. "You okay there, fella?" he asked. "You tied one on last night. Need a ride? You're far from home, and far from town too."

It hadn't occurred to me that the cemetery wasn't in town at all. I was still miles from Ione proper. I tried to smile at him, aware that I must look as crazy as I felt.

"I guess I might," I said. In the trailer I could see a sleek black horse pressing its face against the slats to look me over. It snorted. The live sound of it, and the rattling of it stamping its hooves against the straw on the floor made me come to attention. "I thought I was going to church. But I don't even know where it is."

I tugged at my thin plaid shirt, a gift from the house before the house had gone quiet, trying to make it look better than it was.

"There's no church in Ione."

I was bewildered. Even the tiniest towns had churches.

"Used to be a town of bears and mountain lions, wild horses," Ralph said. "Now we have people, but only just. This was a walk through the wilderness, not a hundred years ago. Still not too safe out here."

I got into the truck. The horse in the trailer stamped and neighed.

"Hush, you," said Ralph. "She doesn't like newcomers. Gets funny around people from away."

I looked out the sliding window. The mare looked back at me, very close, her eyes golden. I could feel her wet breath on my neck as we made our way down the dirt road, and into town.

Behind the hardware store, there was a fenced corral, with bushes tangled around the feet of the fenceposts, blackberries bending the vines back towards the earth. The horse tore at the fruit as Ralph walked it past.

As he slipped the halter from around the horse's ears, something winked silver in the sun. I rubbed my eyes. The mare's hooves seemed wrong. Then they were right again. She trotted into the corral, giving me one last look. Not a friendly horse.

"Maybe a bit hungover after all, fella?" Ralph asked, and slapped me on the back. "No shame in that, though. Every man's got something he can't resist, even when he might know better."

No. It might have been easier if I could have blamed that particular demon for Row's death, instead of my own unseeing carelessness. Carelessness is hard word to live with, when it comes to the thing you care for most. The police had ruled me not to blame, though I tried to surrender. To volunteer.

"You made a horrible mistake, Mr. Mays," the district attorney told me, "but you didn't break the law. You threw yourself on the mercy of the system, and the system rules the death accidental. Accidents can have tragic results, but that doesn't make them crimes."

I stood in that office, my wrists aching for handcuffs, my neck aching for a hangman's noose, my wife standing there too, her rage wrapping around me. I think she wanted to be punished as much as I did, but Row was dead because of me.

I was the one who'd turned the key in the ignition, not Amina. She'd stood on the porch screaming me on my way, and neither of us checked Row's bedroom door, though we both knew he woke when we fought. Row had run out into the night once before, during one of our big blow-ups. In the morning, frantic, we'd found him sleeping in a treetop, draped in the spreading branches of the oak like a bright bird, his costume torn, his crown bent, his thumb in his mouth.

Amina blamed herself for his death as much as she blamed me. I blamed her too, and god, and fate, and stupidity, and my history, and my future, and the town we lived in, and the staircase, and the road, and electricity, and nightfall, and the sun, and the stars, but mostly I blamed myself.

I was the one who'd slam-braked the car at the bottom of the hill, thinking rabbit, deer, cat, dog. I was the one who'd found Row, blood from the corner of his mouth. I was the one who'd carried him home, screaming. No phone—I'd thrown it out the car window as I pulled out of the driveway, giving her no way to find me.

I was the one my wife had met on the porch in the middle of the night, and in my arms, our child, not sleeping. I hadn't killed myself after the ruling, only because I'd heard my grandmother in my head.

"Nothing's for nothing, Malcolm," she'd said to me once when I was down and out, twenty years old, washed up on her porch, trying to recover from a girl I'd lost, telling her I wanted to die. "I have skill made of hard times. Nobody who hasn't been hurt can work a miracle. You have to lose something to know what you have. You think you'll die of love, but you won't. Broken love's not like broken glass. It's like dull, heavy metal. Forge it into something useful, and stop moaning over how the world did you wrong."

My gran cuffed me in the head like a mother cat batting a stupid kitten, and handed me a glass of sweet tea. My granddad laughed from the porch swing. "She doesn't have much in the way of sympathy, boy," he called out. "You came to the wrong woman for that."

But I'd seen her heal a broken-backed goat. I'd seen her fix a car engine by touching it. She wasn't a witch, my gran, but she was known for fixing things.

The night Row died, she was all I could think of, but she was gone fifteen years by then, and my granddad too. I hadn't inherited any of what she knew, and I hadn't bothered to learn it. All I had was the power to break. I knew she would have said that everyone born on earth started out liking the breaking of things more than the fixing of them. The point of growing up was to spend some years fixing before we started breaking again. My gran believed a person's history mattered, that bad history could become something of use, if you paid attention, if you learned.

I'd thought I was on the way to church, but there was another place I hadn't been. Salem was two hundred miles away, but I could do it in a few hours.

I stood there, in the hardware lot, thinking about it, scared and exhilarated at once.

"Are you a handy sort of fella, or will you be looking to hire out the work when you fix up the house?" Ralph startled me, unlocking the dented metal door at the back.

It was my house. "I want to do what I can myself."

The door clanged shut behind us. "All right then. We can start you an account, so all you have to worry about is the reckoning, when it's finished."

I walked slowly through the hardware store. I'd need more paint, I knew. I shoved my hands into the loose pockets of my overalls. In each, cloth wrapped around metal. The horseshoes. They would need nails.

No. I would need nails. Not for horseshoes, but for carpentry. There were boards to be replaced, and the shutters hung off-true, and trim that needed to be tacked back down.

The popcorn maker whirred and snapped into life, and the scent of hot butter and salt filled the store.

"You don't need to take care of all your obligations to the homestead at once," Ralph said. "Give yourself some time to settle in, really get to know the place. Better to know something's true character, than to have to come back and redo mistakes."

Paint, both the white for the walls, and dark blue, for the shutters I would rehang. Nails. Iron nails, not Naglfar's, and not for shoes. Spackle, to fill in holes in the walls where keys had been. Some wood, of varying sizes.

"Is there something that will fix the ground?" I asked Ralph as he rang up my supplies. "Where it's been burned?"

"Seems like a cursed place. Don't know that anything will ever grow there, no matter what you do." He shook his head.

"Do you believe in that sort of thing? Curses?"

Easier to think that too, that I was cursed to break things, rather than that I had broken them by being who I was.

"Someplace like that, with all of what's happened there, if it hadn't already burned to the ground, I'd say that's what should be done. I knew Olivia Weyland. She didn't deserve any of what happened to her. She tried to fix things."

He hadn't answered my question, but I didn't ask it again.

"What's the best way to get to Salem?" I asked instead. He looked me dead in the eye for a moment.

"Well. If you're going to Salem," he said, "you should borrow Lischen's truck. It's out there in the lot. She won't mind. You've got an errand to do."

"I do," I said. "I—"

I almost asked him to go with me, but something in his look told me that was not welcome. He handed me a bag of popcorn and hauled the lumber and supplies out to Lischen's truck.

"It's a drive," he said. "But you might as well get it over."

"Get what over?" I asked.

"Whatever needs doing," Ralph said. "Plenty to do in Salem." He smiled at me, and I got into the pickup. He pointed off into the distance.

"Just go that way about four hours," he said, "until you start smelling the ocean. You see waves, you've gone too far. They'd never put the prisoners where they could see the way to the water. People used to hop the walls. Now they've got barbed wire, and nobody climbs out. Ask me, they should have put the Pen on the coast, or offshore. Like a lighthouse. No pirates on the Oregon coast these days to pick prisoners up. They'd be trapped there with rocks to their backs and sea to the front, and that's a good prison."

Ralph looked ruminatively off into the distance as though he was picturing the prison even as he spoke to me.

"Will they let me in?"

Ralph laughed. "You worried you'll have to break in? No. It's a place like any other, Malcolm. And your errand won't take long."

14.

I stopped by the library to make sure Ralph had been right when he handed me Lischen's spare keys. The doors were locked there, though, and there was no movement inside, despite her saying she'd be working.

The interior of the truck smelled of her perfume. I nearly turned back. It was Sunday, after all. Chances were there'd be no visiting. I could go home, to my safe little house, where no one could find me.

For another two days, anyway. No. I had to go to the prison. *Approved.*

I did go home for a moment, and grabbed a stash of letters, but I took off from the front door without looking back, afraid I wouldn't manage to leave if I considered it any more.

I hit the highway and headed north to I-84, cursing the strangeness of Oregon, the 55 mph speed limit that anywhere else would be 75. It was already mid-morning, and I worried I wouldn't get into the prison before it closed. I should have called. My mind had gotten soft here, and now I expected the rest of the world to feed me lunch and tuck me into bed. It felt good to take the ramp out of town.

I worried my way west, driving a parched landscape, patches of trees as I moved toward Portland, and then, green and dark everywhere. A national forest, so lush it seemed impossible after all the desert. Beside the highway, the river gleamed silver as chains. I looked to the left and saw Mt. Hood, the volcano rising up, snow like a cape over its shoulders. Bridal Veil Falls, a flash of white, a sign announcing a landmark.

I was breathing again, feeling like a real person again. Other cars around me, towns, people. I was driving. I was okay. Nothing was wrong now, not really. I believed, for a moment, that I'd moved on, and then I remembered I was driving toward a prison.

They'd tell me he was dead, and that I was only getting letters as a formality. They'd tell me I needed to pay for his burial. I'd get a motel room, and watch cable TV. I saw signs advertising rooms for $29 a night, old neon with cowboys on them. A motel, a swimming pool, an orange soda. That was what I'd find once this was done. A reward for making sure. That's all I was doing. Making sure.

The prison itself, when I finally got to it, was weirdly beautiful. I'd imagined concrete blocks, and instead it was Art Deco curves, a watchtower rising over the front entrance, and tall arched windows lined with dark tiles. The sun hit the complex in a way that tricked my eyes into thinking I was somewhere nice, a hotel not terribly far from the seaside, maybe, except for the loops of barbed wire around the tops of the walls. The gates were open, to my surprise. I'd expected to fail. The guard motioned a window roll-down, and I struggled with it for a moment, unused to the manual operation in Lischen's truck, but then got it down, and tried to look not guilty. Why? I wasn't guilty.

The guard looked at me, sighed, and said, "Visiting hours are over, mister."

"I need to see the warden," I said, that notion falling out of my mouth unexpectedly.

"There's procedures," the guard said. I looked at the wad of gum he was nursing in his cheek. Bright pink. I could smell the strawberry on his breath. He looked barely old enough to be out of high school, and he'd shaved badly. His face was nicked.

"I need to see him," I said, and pulled the sheaf of letters out of the glove compartment. The guard looked at them, grimacing.

"I don't know what you got here," he said. "But it looks like a mess."

"Letters from a prisoner. From this prison. They're threats," I said, to make it stick.

The guard sighed and blew a bubble, giving up on me. "You can go and see what you get in there," he said. "But nothing goes out without getting read. Can't be much too bad in them. Most guys just write porn to girls. I don't know why you got a guy writing to you, unless those are porn."

He looked at me, curious now. "You getting porn from someone in here? That what's wrong?"

"No. Do you recognize his name?"

The guard looked at the envelope again, at Dusha's name and at my address. "I think I'd remember that one," he said. "But I haven't been here long. There are records in the office. Might be for nothing, and you drove a long way. I used to play basketball near Ione, in high school. That place doesn't even got a team."

He waved me through the gate, and pointed at the lot.

There was a sign in blue paint on the wall outside the front prison office, a layer of bullet glass, and a receptionist behind that, who had no interest in looking up at me.

I stood for several minutes, reading the sign over and over again, like a mantra. *"You can't talk your way out of problems that you behaved your way into."* I wondered why those instructions were facing prison guests, rather than prisoners.

The receptionist looked up, at long last. I could see from the lines of her face that she spent her time behind that glass biting the insides of her cheeks out of boredom, or disgust.

"You don't think you're here for a prisoner visit, do you? You're not on any of my lists."

"I didn't tell you my name."

"Well, you missed basic visiting hours, and there aren't any specials scheduled, so you can assume I know how to do my job."

I pushed the letters through the slot in the glass. She looked at them, with a complicated expression on her face. One part excitement, one part revulsion. She was thinking I had a pile of porn again, I suspected. When she looked up, that expression was gone.

"No one by that name here," she said.

"I've been getting them, sometimes a five or six a day," I said. "Somebody's sending them."

"We control mail in and out," she said. "These are stamped, but this isn't our prisoner. Not ours. He's not on record."

I looked at her.

"That's true," I said. "He's not. He died in 1957." Her face changed. "He was executed. I'm here to pick up his bones."

She sighed. "Some people are fools. Leave well enough alone, but no. You think you'll sell a dead man's bones on eBay? There's a prison cemetery here, and if he's dead and nobody claimed him, he's in it. What you're doing here sixty years late, I don't know."

"I'm not leaving until I see someone. I want to pick up his bones. And I want these letters explained."

"Do you know where you are?"

"The penitentiary," I said.

"Then don't fuck with me," she replied, startling me. "Don't threaten, don't pretend I can't throw you out if I want to. Prisons aren't for tourists. The only reason you're getting this far is that it's the end of the day and nobody has procedure for this."

She slammed the door behind her as she went deeper into the prison. I waited to be thrown out. Guards with guns? This didn't seem like a prison to me. It seemed like a post office, and the receptionist an irritable postal worker.

A door opened across the room.

"Malcolm Mays?" The man beckoned to me. Khaki uniform, badge. Maybe in his sixties, with teeth that looked older. His skin was as though he'd pulled the plug partway on an air mattress, before realizing he didn't want to go flat. "You're wanted."

"I was cleared," I said, without even thinking of what I was saying.

He looked at me.

"Wanted back here," he said, and beckoned again. "It's the end of the day, and I'm due home for Sunday supper. Just come with me."

My spine felt like a spring. I couldn't decide whether to go back beyond that door with him, or to leave, claiming confusion. He decided for me. He grabbed the letters from my hand, and looked at them.

"You're coming with me," he said. "I'm Warden Kern, and you've got some explaining to do. Thank you, Lois."

The receptionist shot me a triumphant look as I went into the prison itself. On the warden's belt, I could see a holster. The door clanged shut behind us, and a red light came on above it. He saw me looking.

"Security," he said. "This is a prison. What do you have there, Malcolm Mays?"

"How do you know my name?"

"It's right here on these letters, isn't it? It is."

He led me into an office, and slammed the door, dropping into a soft desk chair while I sat awkwardly in aluminum. He looked hard at me.

"And I know these letters. I wondered if you were real."

"Who did you think they were going to?"

"What are you trying to do here, Mays? You're in my house now. I'm two years out from the end of my sentence."

"What did you say?"

"Retirement," he said. "This place is a sentence like anything else. I have a man ready to come up and sit where I sit. I have grandkids. Tell me what you want, I'll tell you what you can't have, and you can be on your way."

"I want to see Dusha Chuchonnyhoof," I said.

"Deceased," he said. "In 1957. Executed by gas chamber. You know that already. You said it out there."

"He's not dead," I said. "He's haunting my house. Or, not my house. Haunting my mail."

The warden's lip curled. "He's dead."

I brought out Olivia's letter about the executions, and pushed it across the desk. He looked at it, at first cursorily, and then less so. At last, having brought out a cigarette lighter, and set the letter on fire, the warden spoke again.

"Leave this alone. Get up from that seat, walk out to the lot, and leave this the hell alone."

"He's asking me to help him."

"Dusha Chuchonnyhoof is legally dead," the warden repeated, looking me in the eyes. "He was executed. By the power of the state, at the end of his sentence. There were witnesses. His death certificate was signed. And he's buried in the cemetery here."

"What if he didn't die?"

The warden's hand moved toward his holster.

"This is my prison, Mays. I'd know. And if I knew we had a prisoner here, a prisoner who wouldn't die? It would be my business what I did with that prisoner. If that prisoner wrote letters, if that was part of the condition of his imprisonment, if that prisoner were passed to me by the warden before me, and by the warden before him, if all of us had been waiting a HUNDRED AND SEVENTEEN FUCKING YEARS for that goddamned prisoner to be released? Do you think I'd fuck it up, Mays? Do you think I'd let him out into the world before his sentence was over? Do you think I'd surrender my prisoner to you?"

The warden's hand was on his gun.

"Where is he?" I tried. "Can I see him? I don't have to talk to—"

"Dead, Mays. Dusha Chuchonnyhoof is dead. No one sees him. You can't go gape at a dead man."

The extra flesh on the warden's face now seemed filled with something that might make him levitate, a mascot from a balloon parade gone small in this office.

"There will be no scandal here, Mays, hear me? If we had a prisoner here, if we did, a prisoner who wouldn't die? We wouldn't want the world to know, would we? There'll be a moment when this all comes right and we're waiting for that moment. A couple days left in that sentence. This is a job. I don't truck with the devil in here. I don't owe the devil my soul."

Suddenly he was over the desk at me, his gun in his hand.

"If I find you got leaky lips, I can help you with that. A warden is authorized."

The click of the safety.

"You ready to leave my prison now?"

I was.

"Lois will let you out."

Lois took me to the parking lot, and watched while I got into the truck. She watched while I drove out the gates, and away in the dark.

Dusha Chuchonnyhoof was alive, real, and in that prison. He wasn't invented. There seemed to be nothing I could do about it.

He was coming home to me.

15.

As I turned into the dirt lane at dawn, the truck caught on something. There was a bang, and the wheel jerked sideways in my hand. It fishtailed to a stop. I sat, shaking. There hadn't been a bump. I hadn't hit anything. Anyone. Not this time.

The front tire on the passenger side had blown.

I looked everywhere to see what it had caught on, but found no rock, no litter from the yard, no tossed-aside piece of lumber with nails still sticking out. I couldn't find the spare, either, so I heaved some of the paint, nails, and two-by-fours out of the truck bed, and hauled them back to the house.

A letter cartwheeled from the ceiling to land at my feet. I picked it up, intending to just pile it up with the others and burn the whole heap later, but it was the stationery and handwriting I had come to think of as Olivia's. Whatever it said, I felt I owed it to her to read it.

October 31

Dear Malcolm,

Forgive my brevity, but it is difficult to write. The walls are thin, but not yet open, and your stubbornness, Malcolm, does not help.

So that you may know it is me, I will say that you were brought a gift yesterday morning. Popovers. You might reconsider eating them.

Dusha Chuchonnyhoof is neither a demon, nor your enemy. I do not know if there is a Heaven or a Hell, nor do I know if I am to go anywhere beyond where I am now, in the house, but I am still a Christian ~~woman~~ *soul, and I would not advise anyone to take a path that might lead them into* ~~Hell~~ *torment.*

Help Dusha. Do what is necessary, no matter how strange it seems. Tell him you will help, agree to the terms, and those of us remaining in the house will be able to help you again. We want to. I want to ~~and I wish to be free of this life which is not a life no matter where it is I might go after.~~

~~We will protect you. Trust that it will be well.~~
I still hold out hope of Heaven.

The End of the Sentence

Soon, Malcolm.
Please.

Olivia Jones Weyland

I did not want to be in debt to a murderer, (though again, the thought pinched at me. I was guilty and free. What if he was innocent and caged?) and God knew I didn't want to commit murders of my own. I already knew what it was to carry the burden of a death.

But I wanted to help Olivia. If I could free her, I had a duty to do so. Maybe I'd misunderstood what was being asked of me. I'd misunderstood things in my life before, and maybe more than I'd known. I heard my grandmother again, and I thought about fixing things other than the ones I'd broken. She hadn't been the one who broke that goat's back. She hadn't broken the car engine, but she'd fixed them, all the same.

I turned the letter over.

Same day

Chuchonnyhoof,

I'm not doing this for you. And this is my house, not yours, but if you must come here, then you must. I will give what help I can.

I read over the words. I hadn't promised to kill anyone, to cut off hands. I would help, if I could. That wasn't
a lie. I wouldn't promise further.

Malcolm Mays

I set it outside on the porch where I'd put the previous
letter. I didn't know what answer I wanted.

The smell of coffee crept out from the kitchen and
down the hall. I heard the sizzle of grease on a hot skillet,
and the clank of glass bottles rattling in the shelves of a
refrigerator door. The house, at least, had forgiven me.

The plate was heaped with bacon, eggs and hash-
browns. It smelled good, and I wasn't in the habit of
turning down food. Leaning against a glass of orange
juice was a letter from the prison. *Approved.*

Thirty-first October

My dear Malcolm,

*Forgive me my temper and my silence. Under-
stand that your first letter came to me at a time
where I could very nearly taste my freedom, could
smell the rain-soaked earth and sky, and feel the
breeze upon my skin. To have the one person I was
counting on suddenly and cruelly refuse to offer*

*me any aid when I had been nothing but kind and
generous, hurt more than I can say, Malcolm.*

*But no matter. I understand what it is to fear,
what it is to fall under the sway of evil counsel, how
even the kindest word can sound wrong to an ear
filled with suspicion. Stop your ears against those who
would seek to turn you from me, Malcolm.*

*I am grateful. You have returned to me, and of
your own free will. Our bond is strengthened by this,
and so the binding will be an easier thing to perform.*

*I return to you soon, as I must. Complete the
binding, Malcolm. I have no wish to become a monster. It is your actions that will ensure that I do not.*

Dusha.

I couldn't make the two sides match up in my head.
Olivia wanted me to help. She would help me, protect
me, if I did. But the thing she wanted me to help was a
monster who, as far as I could tell, had not changed his
demand that I murder two people and forge their hands
into shoes for him. He might not want to be a monster,
but he seemed bent on making me one. And no matter
what anyone said, the dead didn't come back to life. Dead
wasn't the kind of thing that could be fixed.

Behind me, water splashed into the sink. A woman's
voice, humming. "My Baby Cares Just for Me."

I carried the paint and spackle upstairs. There was work I could do, clean work, that didn't mean walking down dark stairs and lighting a fire in a forge.

The outline of the red door had bled further through the paint, and the key was once again sticking out of the wall. The pencil on the nightstand lifted up into the air and floated across the room. *O-P-E-N* scrawled in loose letters above the key.

"It's not a door," I said.

OPEN. The pencil underlined the letters, pressing so hard the lead snapped. It was the first time I'd seen things actually moving in the air. The ghosts didn't care any longer whether I saw them moving about.

I turned the key, and felt it catch tumblers. Click.

The door opened into a space behind my bedroom wall. There were shelves, like a pantry, but not for holding food. On the shelves were six pair of horseshoes. No— six and a half. Thirteen total.

I felt like I was standing before a crypt. The horseshoes rested together in their pairs, the hands of each lover. The bottoms of them were worn, rubbed smooth in places, scratched and nicked in others. Some of the hands wore wedding bands. In one instance, both hands were small, delicate-fingered, with long nails, as if both belonged to women.

Only the solitary shoe showed no sign of being worn. I had two horseshoes—the beautiful one, that had been left on the anvil's horn, and the ragged one that had risen out of the dirt to grip my hand. Perhaps one of them was the mate, but I didn't know how to tell, and it seemed wrong, to match up a pair that wasn't true.

There was one more thing, heaped in a corner of a shelf. It was so tarnished that at first I thought it was iron, too. But no. Too light, and the metal near white when I scraped at it. Silver. A bridle made of silver. Even the reins, dangling from the bit.

I sat down in the doorway that wasn't, and thought about what I could do, what I couldn't do, what I didn't know. I thought about who that bridle might be meant to fit. Maybe there was a horse waiting for me, like that mare. I wasn't from horse country. I didn't know anything about riding. I didn't know anything about horseshoes, even now, and as I thought it, I nearly laughed with misery. I was only a month into a new life. How was it that I was supposed to know everything? How was it that these were the stakes? *Tell him you will help.*

Hands holding hooves. Whose hooves? What *was* Dusha Chuchonnyhoof? No one had told me that, for all that there were threats and vows and promises. No one had said what sort of creature he was. *No one sees him,* Warden Kern had said. No one had described the goblin I was meant to keep bound. No one had told me why he needed binding.

The bedroom window was open and I could smell fall coming in, leaves beginning to crumble into dust. There was a cool breeze hitting the back of my neck, but in the closet it was hot as a forge.

Beneath each of the sets of shoes, there was a letter.

No, not a letter. A contract.

The first one was written out in fading brown ink, the handwriting unfamiliar to me. It had a location too, *Gretna Green, Scotland.*

I picked the paper up from the shelf, and shuddered. Beneath it, there was a long braid of hair, two different sorts. One red, one black, twisted into a coil and tied with a faded string.

> *Samira Eld is wedded to Theodore Miller this first of November, in the year of our lord seventeen hundred and fifty-four. Witnessed by the blacksmith priest, the former trapper and New World traveler Joseph Weyland, in the blacksmith's shop at Gretna Green, upon the wedding anvil belonging to this shop. The anvil is rung by the blacksmith priest, and these two are handfasted, promised by their fingers and by their blood to one another, and to their witness, a man of this town, brother-in-marriage (now bereaved) to this blacksmith, who shall watch over them, and in deeds, repay them their gifts.*

Beneath that, the signatures of the couple, the signature of Joseph Weyland, and a mark. The C and W brand.

The End of the Sentence

Followed by the signature of the wedding's witness. The flowing looping lines, the dark ink, the handwriting I knew all too well.

> *With this hammer and this anvil, with this promise, I take your hands to mine,*

the last line of the contract read, and then, it was signed.

Dusha Chuchonnyhoof.

16.

I went through the rest of the contracts quickly. Name after name, each one witnessed (witnessed or much more?) by Chuchonnyhoof. Centuries of marriages.

The weddings moved from Scotland to the deck of *Glashtyn*, a ship somewhere on the Atlantic Ocean. I quivered, imagining a monster aboard a ship, though what monster I still didn't know. Hooves on a deck. Two hooves, not four. There were never four shoes, and it was only now that I considered that. A picture of Dusha Chuchonnyhoof assembled itself in my mind, hooves on animal legs, a man's muscled torso.

The next wedding was in Massachusetts, the two women, and I thought about that for a moment, the time that this had occurred, and the place. Inez Weyland and Isabella Fuller. At last, the anvil seemed to have shifted to the Oregon Territory, where, for a hundred eighty years and more, the anvil weddings had been, it seemed, taking place here, at the blacksmith's shop in Ione.

It dawned on me that *blacksmith's shop in Ione* meant my house. The anvil below this property was the anvil upon which these weddings had been performed.

Beneath some of the contracts, there were other items. I found a pocketwatch with a locket containing a delicate portrait in watercolor, a beautiful woman whose face reminded me of Lischen's, the entirety of the image no larger than my fingerprint. All of the contracts had locks of hair, braided together, presumably from the married couple.

They'd all taken place on the first of November. Beginning in America, some of the contracts had additional clauses.

> *Robert March is wedded to Annika Miller, this first of November, in the year of our lord eighteen hundred and three. Witnessed by the blacksmith priest, Marvel Weyland, here in the blacksmith's shop at Ione, in the Oregon Territory, over the wedding anvil belonging to this shop. The anvil is rung by the blacksmith priest, and these two are handfasted, promised by their fingers and by their blood to one another, and to their witness, who shall watch over them, and in deeds, repay them their gifts.*

The End of the Sentence

For Annika Miller: a hand that may bring fruit to the trees here in this desert.

For Robert March: a diviner's hand, water called to his fingertips when the wells run dry and the rains do not come.

With this hammer and this anvil, with this promise, I take your hands to mine:

Dusha Chuchonnyhoof

The promises in writing, impossible promises. My mind was ringing with the words I'd heard from Dusha. *If you do as I tell you to do, he will return when I do.*

For Malcolm Mays: the return of Rowan Mays, his son, thought dead.

Except that he asked you to be the smith, I thought, and the smith performs the weddings. He didn't ask you to marry over the anvil. You're not a young lover. You're not young and there's no one for you in Ione. Was I meant to perform all the functions? The smith and the lovers both? Surely not. It wasn't possible. That was what Olivia had tried to do.

There was no mention of payment to the smith in these contracts. Just in the first one, the mention of the brother-in-law, Dusha married to the sister of the blacksmith Joseph Weyland. *Now bereaved.*

Former trapper and New World traveler, it said, too, next to Weyland's name, and I looked at the date again, thought about what someone with those credentials might have been doing in the middle of the 1700s. A blurry Lewis and Clark memory, and of the people who'd come decades before them, the wandering trappers who'd brought home furs. Homestead, Dusha called this. Maybe he'd come from here to begin with, traveled to Scotland with the trapper, and then returned.

I looked around wildly. There was no original set of shoes, nor anything else that might mark that first wedding. The first anvil wedding, it must be, that of Dusha Chuchonnyhoof to a woman named Weyland. Who was she? Did he grieve her?

What was she?

"Who was she?" I said aloud, asking the house. "Who did he love?"

A gust of cold wind under the rattling window-frame, and with that wind, a stinging ice. I turned and looked into the bedroom. On the floor, a word written in hailstones.

ABIGAYL

Into the room fluttered a small pamphlet. The Worshipful Company of Blacksmiths, it said, in crabbed script. A roster of smiths, for the year 1725. It went on to say that the company contained sixty-four brethren, and two sistren. I ran my finger down the list until I found her. *Abigayl Weyland.*

Chuchonnyhoof's wife, a blacksmith, a Weyland. *Now bereaved.*

A vision again, a tent in the winter, hooves outside, a trapper inside it, trying to sleep. A case of hides. Hooves and howling wolves. Pitch black in the tent. Sleeping. Hooves and howls.

I watched the trapper wake to a set of blue eyes staring at him from the dark. I watched a wedding, a woman in a blacksmith's apron, and this man, this Joseph Weyland, performing a ceremony for his sister and the thing he'd brought back from the Americas.

She'd died. Something had happened that sent Chuchonnyhoof in desperate search of shoes. Maybe she'd kept him shod, but with what? What was she? Only a blacksmith or more than that? Nearly a hundred and fifty years had passed after her death, with Chuchonnyhoof still living, before the crime he'd been jailed for.

What had happened with Lischen March and Michael Miller? What had gone wrong?

There was just the one shoe left alone on the shelf. It was half the size of the rest, and with it there was no contract, no lock of braided hair. Beneath it, only a small note written on a scrap of cloth. November, 1900, and a name, or a word, I didn't know which. *Hew.*

I went to the set of horseshoes before the last, solitary one. I picked up the contract beneath it, and found what I'd glimpsed earlier. This contract was dated 1876, between Elkanah March and Lischen Wildshoe.

A daguerreotype of a couple. I looked at their faces, not smiling, but looking straight at the camera, the way those old photos always were, posed and stiff. The girl seemed to be Native American, but dressed in the clothing of a white woman. She had brown skin, black eyes, a high lace collar fastened with a cameo, black hair tightly parted in the center, and a familiar face, one corner of her mouth bent upward like a hairpin. I looked closer. The man was white, and older than his bride, close-cropped hair, a beard, a string tie.

Each of them had a bracelet tightly fastened around their left wrist. A silver bracelet in the shape of clasped hands. I knew those bracelets. I'd seen one worn.

Dusha's promises on that contract:

For Lischen Wildshoe: a hand to tame all horses.
For Elkanah March: a hand to tame all horses.

I looked again at the solitary shoe and saw what was different about it. The fingers weren't right. They were tiny, and they were strange, too smooth, without fingerprints. These fingers weren't human, or not entirely.

17.

Rain spat its way into the room. I froze, my hands on the warped wood of the windowframe, my nerves flaming like arrows shot over a wall.

There was a horse at the end of my property, out by Lischen's truck. Black.

I thought it might be the same horse Ralph had with him in the trailer, though I couldn't see the eyes at this distance.

The horse tossed its head up, and then it rippled, collapsing on itself and stretching at the same time. I stared.

Not a horse. A woman. Naked, in the rain and hail, and like a fool, I thought that she must be cold, that I should bring her a blanket. I grabbed one from my bed, and ran down the stairs.

At the door stood Lischen, feet bare and mud-splotched, black hair dripping onto the rain-soaked red dress she wore.

She took the blanket from my hands and wrapped it around her hair. She pushed past me into the hall.

"What did you do to my truck, Malcolm?"

I looked through the open door. No horse. No woman. "The tire blew. I don't know why."

"I do. This place doesn't like me, and the feeling is mutual. Come back inside, Malcolm, and stop looking for what's dripping in your hallway."

"You're a horse." Not as strange as I would have thought it before I came to Ione, to this house. I glanced at her feet.

"Only sometimes. And no. I'm not the thing that needs shoeing." The bracelet, clasped hands in sliver, was tight against her wrist.

"Is the bracelet a family design?"

She smiled, and the hair on the back of my neck stood. "Now, why would you ask a question like that? Did the door open, Malcolm? Did you find the shoes?" She walked to the bottom of the stairs. "It's up here, isn't it?"

Upstairs, a door slammed.

"I told you. The place doesn't like me. You go first— it'll let you in. You live here." She unwrapped the blanket from her hair, and draped it over the banister. A long black hair clung to the fabric.

I wasn't sure I wanted Lischen anywhere the house and its ghosts didn't want her. "That's a strange thing to say, that the place doesn't like you."

"Oh, I know a bit about this house. I've been here a few times, and again, after the last of the Weylands was gone, looking for what was mine. It's not the first time that dirt lane has grown disappearing rocks that last just long enough to pop my tires. I know there are doors that won't open without keys. I told you I had a history, Malcolm. It's here, and I want it back. He doesn't get to have that too."

I thought I knew the answer, but I asked anyway. "Who?"

"The end of the sentence is almost here, and he'll be back, in his new pair of shoes. The monster who killed my son."

She walked up the first couple of steps, then looked back. "Don't just stand there gaping like a landed fish. Show me the door and show me the shoes. I want what's mine." She kicked the wall as she passed it, and the kick rang out like she'd hit it with iron.

"Your son?" I said. That was all I could say. I felt a knot in my chest like a swallowed apple.

"The door," she said.

It hadn't been the bedroom door that slammed shut, but the painted one. The key had fallen out, and was almost hidden beneath the bed.

"I know there's a door there, right in the wall. I'm the one who painted it open," Lischen said. "I came back and visited it the other night, but even with you here, tucked

135

in your bed and me smelling of your sheets, the house wouldn't let me in."

The key stuck, and part of me hoped it wouldn't turn. But the tumblers turned over and I felt the lock open. The door cracked. I could refuse. Lock it back up, and not open it until I had my answers. The house would help.

But, her child. If there was even a piece of truth in that. I thought of my own son, my Row, in dress and crown.

I opened the door.

Her eyes came to rest on the solitary shoe. She made a sound I couldn't identify, a gasping choke. "There," she said. "There. He made a shoe, after all. I knew it. He couldn't let it go. He couldn't let him go. The monster. I trusted him, and he—"

She looked at me, her eyes liquid around golden pupils.

"I trusted him," Lischen said. "But trust is nothing, Malcolm." She reached out a fingertip and grazed it over the solitary shoe, then yanked her hand away as if it was red hot.

I could smell her now, cedar, forest, and tarnished silver, and wondered at how I'd been unable to identify it. Of course she was the one who'd been in my room.

"The bracelet," I stammered. "There's a picture of a couple, with that set of shoes, there, and they're wearing the same ones. The woman's named Lischen, so I was wondering if it had some meaning."

"You really should have spent more time in the library, Malcolm. You are what you are, and I am too. You have your own stories, and I don't know them." She looked at me, and corrected herself. "I don't know them all."

I felt transparent. What *did* she know of me?

"When the Weylands came to Ione, they brought their anvil with them. They made their living as blacksmiths. They brought the tradition of the anvil marriage with them, too. A smith could pronounce a couple married and have it be just as binding as the words said by a minister. They brought one more thing. Dusha Chuchonnyhoof was part of their family. He came from the mountains here to begin with, called by another name back then, by the people who'd been here thousands of years. He'd vowed himself to a Weyland, way back, and married that man's sister, and now he was bound to them.

"There were promises made. The Weylands would give him their hands, and he would give them what they needed."

"Their actual hands," I said.

"Don't ask questions you already know the answers to. It was a trade. And when the marriage was solemnized over the anvil, new hands were struck on. The Weylands were no longer the materials. The shoes were made of volunteers. Like me." She held up her left hand, so that the bracelet gleamed.

"My parents made the bargain. That's them in the picture. My Mom became a whitesmith, and she taught me her craft. My Dad was a trader—Ralph's used to be his general store."

She stopped at that, and looked at me. Her eyes were very golden now.

"Nine months after their anvil marriage, Elkanah March and Lischen Wildshoe had a child. My inheritance came from her family. It had made them powerful in their tribe, and then, later, when the world changed, become a terrible secret. My mother was afraid that when she had a child, the child might inherit it, even though she had not, and so my parents gave their hands to Dusha, and he gave them, you've read it—"

"The power to tame horses," I said.

"Good student, for all you're slow," said Lischen. "Every night I knelt beside my bed to pray, and every night my parents took my hands in theirs. Their touch kept me human. I didn't know what I was until I was three and twenty."

She took the portrait of her parents from the shelf and shoved it at me.

"Look at them. They bargained with a beast. There are punishments for that. Sometimes punishments are slow."

The composure she'd had for a moment was gone. Her eyes were nothing human. In the dark of the not-closet, they glowed. I had a wild thought, instructions from childhood, from my grandparents, whose land lay beside a tangle of trees. 'Stand still, Malcolm. Don't run from a predator,' and though Lischen was neither panther nor bear, I had to force myself to remain standing. I thought of something from one of those old stories, a horse that led you into the woods, and then left your bones. The people in those stories had gone willingly.

"What happened?" I said.

Lischen picked up the solitary shoe in her braceleted hand, wincing, balancing it carefully in the center of her palm. I wasn't sure I wanted to know anything else from this woman I felt both moved and frightened by. The small shoe in her palm looked even stranger as I looked at it, less like human fingers made metal, more like a hoof itself, a hoof with finger nubs, its center hollowed. It was nothing like the rest of the horseshoes. It was horse, or half-horse.

Lischen shrugged, and unexpectedly laughed.

"I fell in love, Malcolm. You should have known that much. I went out walking in the dark one night, looking at the stars, and I remembered the blackberries that grew behind this old house. I thought to steal some. I didn't think Ironhide really existed. Some story told to keep us from bothering the house, the monster who protected the boundary. This, I knew, was where Marvel Weyland lived, and my parents came here to get our horses shod. They wore their bracelets. I didn't know what they'd done. I never saw their wrists without their cuffs. You'll never see mine."

She looked at me pleadingly.

"How could I have known? He was standing in the dark outside the back door when I first saw him. In those days, the mint was high around the porch and there were violets blooming year round. The tree in front of the house bore peaches, plums, nectarines and apricots, all at the same time, the project of some crazy grafter. This town was full of things to wonder about. There were farmers who harvested their crops in January, and diviners who brought water from the salt flats. Ione had people who could build houses without nails, and people who could heal cancer using their fingertips. But I came from here. Wonders were what I knew.

"I'd never seen him before, and I knew everyone. I thought about running, but there was no reason for me to run. He was my neighbor, and I was only being neighborly, though I felt shy looking at him. He was shirtless, his skin tanned. His eyes were the blue of skimmed milk. I could see them, and his smile in the dark. Once I saw those things, I knew I wouldn't forget them.

"'What kind of thing are you?'" he asked me.

"'Lischen March,'" I said.

"'No, *what?*'" he asked. "'Not who. What kind of thing are you?'"

In the hidden closet, next to this woman who was telling me a story of something that had happened a hundred and seventeen years earlier, (which made her a hundred and forty, oh Malcolm, what dreams are these?) I felt it unroll in front of my eyes, a scroll of images. Lischen in a long white nightdress in the back yard, her lips stained with juice, her black hair, streaming to her waist, and her eyes, glowing. In the vision, there was no cuff on her wrist, and it seemed too intimate. Like looking at someone else's bride on her wedding night. I couldn't see Dusha. I could only see his eyes. The house felt nervous around me, the walls shaking slightly, but somehow I was being given these images, like a movie playing inside the closet.

"'I'm Lischen. I'm a whitesmith,' I said to the man. 'I didn't mean to steal your fruit. I'll pay you in silver, if you like. I'll pay you for your loss.'

"He laughed. 'If you could do that, you'd be more than anyone else in the world. But even lacking that, you're more than you think you are,' the man said, and lay his hand on mine. It was then I felt it.

"I changed into what I'd been always, kept from it all those years by my parents. I stood in front of Dusha for the first time, what I really am. We were not the same, he and I, but we had things in common."

Lischen looked at me, a keen, dangerous look. "Maybe you know something about that sort of thing, Malcolm Mays, or why are you here? Nobody comes here that wasn't called, Malcolm. You got called by someone."

Lischen walked back into the bedroom, looking around with certainty as though everything in the house was her own, the bed, the walls, the floors, the sheets, and maybe me along with them.

"I used to come here at night, after that," she said. "I used to sleep in his bed, this bed. I counted him my husband. Maybe he loved me, and maybe he didn't. He was known in these parts, but not for what he really was. Neither was I. People called him Ironhide for what he'd said at some point was a family illness, his blood oxidizing his body. He was rusting, but he wore the shoes, and they kept him human enough to pass. The ones my parents had given him were wearing thin by the time I met him. He needed a new set of volunteers, but he told me I was the one he'd been waiting for. Dusha Chuchonnyhoof sank when he swam, and in the rain, his skin turned red. He stayed indoors during the day, mostly, but in the dark, we gloried. We ran in the hills outside of town, he and I, and even shod, he can run like—"

"Like what," I managed. "What is he?"

She looked at me. That hairpin curl at the corner of her mouth, a bent smile, rage locked in the bend.

"A monster," she said. "He's a monster. But the monster fathered my son. In the dark, Malcolm, you can love a monster easily enough. In the dark, you can hold a monster in your arms. Maybe you know something about that."

"I don't know what you mean," I said.

"Then maybe you were the monster," said Lischen, and smiled at me. Her teeth were too pointed. "You had a wife, didn't you? Maybe your wife was the one who didn't see what you were until it was too late. You had a son. What did you do to your son, Malcolm Mays?"

I had nothing to say. There was nothing to tell her.

She knew it already. She was pulling out a photograph, printed from the newspaper accounts of the trial. My little boy, dressed in his shining clothes, the photo that had been splashed out into the world. Some people thought I killed him on purpose, to wish away a life I hadn't wanted.

"Rowan," she said. "Rowan Mays, you left it on the screen in the library. Innocent people don't come to a place like this."

She wasn't saying anything I hadn't said already. I'd shouted the words myself. I was guilty. Guilty deserved a punishment. In her hand, she held the solitary horsehoe.

"You think you deserve a death, but you don't," she said. "I don't either. Look at me, still young enough to marry all over again.

"My parents hid me from the town after I was pregnant. I was Lischen March, the whitesmith, and while I carried my son, I worked silver and my mother wet it with tears. I didn't shift into the horse body. I stayed this, but still, our son was born different. His left hand was a hoof."

I jumped, hearing that, spoken so plainly.

"A hoof. He was something between the two of us, neither human, nor horse. But he was mine. I named him Hew. An old word for heart, not from my mother's people, but from my father's. Dusha told me he could give me what we both wanted, a new hand for our son. But I had to have an anvil wedding. That was the price. Not his price. *The* price.

"We found a man for me to marry. This tiny town, there were only a few options. I'd known Michael since I was a child, and he'd always been kind to me. We'd be wed, and Michael was glad of it. Michael knew there was a child. I didn't lie to him, but he didn't meet Hew until that night at the forge. Hew was two years old, a little thing, hardly in the world yet, but giddy with it, nonetheless. I'd made him a little hand of silver. I didn't ask Dusha for a hand made of flesh. That was more than I could imagine. I only wanted the hoof to go away, and I'd replace it. It was snowing that year, early and all the crops had withered on the vine, but it was hot underground, and Hew was frightened. Marvel Weyland began the ceremony, striking my hand, but Michael Miller, even as his hand was on the anvil, had second thoughts"—she reached out and picked up the solitary horseshoe, and gripped it so hard her knuckled whitened— "he said he would marry me, but that he wouldn't raise another man's child, and especially not a child who'd never be right. Hew was scared of the blood. He thought I was being hurt. He put his hand on the anvil between ours. Marvel Weyland struck it as he swung for Michael's hand. My son died, and Chuchonnyhoof didn't save him."

She paused, clenching her fingers and then unclenching them, her face unreadable.

"I promised him I'd see him in prison for it, and I kept him there. I'm not about to let things be easy for him, now that he's getting out."

I saw it all, the little boy, his malformed hand, Lischen bleeding, the boy bleeding, his hand struck by the hammer, flattened into this little horn of metal. Miller cringing from the monster. And all the while, Dusha Chuchonnyhoof, blue-eyed, stricken, watching.

Lischen weighed the little shoe.

"I don't know where my hand went. Nor do I know what Dusha gave me in return, other than this long life, which I never wanted, and this left hand, which I wear, though it belongs to him. Michael Miller died that day, in the forge. Dusha didn't kill him. I did."

"How?" I asked.

She looked steadily at me. She opened her lips. I could see her teeth again, too sharp, and her eyes glowed, and she was, for a moment, not a horse, not a woman, not a panther, but all of those things at once. You don't run from a predator.

"My child was gone, and I hid myself away. Dusha went to prison for killing me. My family knew about my child, but dared not mention him in the press. Ironhide was the town's secret, but the town turned on him. Now he's coming home. His shoes must be the thinnest metal. He must be in agony. I haven't had a home in a hundred years and more. He took my life and Hew's. All the ghosts who serve this house. He's the one who kept them here. He's no good. He's nothing good."

She looked at me and her lip curled.

"But you know what it is to lose a child. You know."

"Chuchonnyhoof told me he could bring Row back if I helped him. He had a picture. But Row's been dead a year."

She shook her head, drops of cold water falling from her hair. "Maybe he could have done so before, though I offered him both my hands to bring back what was lost, and he told me such a thing was impossible. He'll be weak now, and his skin near totally iron, and he will need the shoes, to stand upon the earth. You can't make those shoes. Not alone. I want my son back. I need one more round of gifts, Malcolm."

We looked at each other.

The clang of the letter flap, opening and closing. Lischen smiled through clenched teeth. "I think that's for you."

18.

My Dear Malcolm,

This will be my last letter to you from this place. I feel as if I should celebrate, but I cannot. I am sure you understand.

And so you know. My shame, my guilt, not for the crime I was jailed for, but for the life of a child that I could not save. His mother blames me, and I blame myself. Love was required, and hers for her child was so strong that I could not see that the man who came with her loved nothing but himself. I loved her too, you know.

I loved, oh I loved, our son.

The curse fell on Michael Miller and his people as hard as it fell on the rest of us. Generation upon generation fallen. Now that all of them are gone, even the earth turns from their graves.

Too much time has passed for me to make all things as they were, but I have not lost what has always been mine.

Tomorrow is the day of my return, and the hour for us both, Malcolm. I will meet you at the boundary of the land. Be ready for what must come.

I heard hooves in the upstairs hallway, hooves on the staircase. I walked to the window. Lischen's red truck and the old car that had come with the house were both gone. I didn't dwell long on the manner of either of their leaving.

Tomorrow is the day of the binding, but I am not the only one bound by the day. There is still help to be looked for.

There is still hope.

Dusha.

Hope. Lischen spoke as if the bargain, the anvil marriage had been commonly known. But so much time had passed—two lifetimes and a day—between then and now that no one would volunteer: "Come, and lay your hands across the anvil, and swear your love to one another in blood. Give me your hands."

There were blackberries covering the kitchen table. Heaped and piled, masses of purple. On the bottom corner of the table, the berries were arranged to spell *Lischen*.

She had said the house didn't like her, but this was a gift. I took the letters out of the reed basket, and put the berries into it. I would bring them to her tomorrow.

There was no such thing as a peace offering. I didn't know what peace she might require. Dusha Chuchonnyhoof's sentence ended hour by hour.

Nerves and adrenalin chased themselves like snakes beneath my skin, and I did not sleep well. I half-dreamt of the heat of a forge and hand. Of poisoned earth, failure and death. Of Row, broken beneath the wheel of my car, and a silver hand in a pool of blood.

Then a noise, a shaking, drums. Louder. I sat up in bed, and could see the door shaking in the wall.

Louder.

The door flew open.

Not drumbeats. Hoofbeats. Each pair of shoes galloping on its shelf. Lifting and falling as if there were hooves in them still. Almost in sync, almost exact, but for the off note of the one solitary shoe, still here. Why had she left it?

It tripped from the edge of its shelf, and fell to the ground. As it hit, the galloping stopped. The only noise the pounding rush of blood in my ears.

The end of the sentence was here.

19.

I could smell smoke drifting in, not just tendrils, but black smoke, darkening the air. The house was not on fire. It came from outside. I didn't know anything about magic and monsters. I was just someone trying to start over.

The house lit lights, brilliant ones, lights I hadn't known existed, and boiled water to a screaming hiss. The house brought a basin, and with it a cloth, a cake of soap, and a razor. The house did not sing any longer, but tapped, ready, waiting for me to be ready alongside it. I felt the presence of Olivia and looked for a letter, but there was nothing.

No, a word, twisting in the steam.

Hope.

I looked at the clock. Midnight, the first moments of November. Was he at the edge of the property? Not yet. He would drive, as I had, from Salem, from the prison.

The smoke was leaves and grass and trees, and the trees were from nowhere around here. Pines from the forests to the north. I could smell their needles. I looked at the solitary horseshoe, and picked it up. Hot, as though it had been galloping down a paved road for miles.

I washed myself, and then saw the clothes the house had left me, pressed and ready. Ceremonial clothes. A suit, old-fashioned, long tails on the jacket and on the shirt, the shirt handstitched in fine cotton. The suit was black wool and handwoven, and the vest the same, lined in indigo silk. I knew where I'd seen them before. On Lischen's father, in the photo in the closet. I looked at the monogram, and yes. The letters EM, elegantly stitched in blood-red thread on the cuffs. As I looked at them, they unraveled and then stitched themselves back again.

MM, said the monogram now. The same initials as Michael Miller, I thought, and then I tried to throw that thought away, an image of him savaged, torn apart.

I put the shirt on. I stopped at the mirror over the dresser and looked at myself for a moment, then picked up something I'd kept from touching all these months since the accident. Row's crown, bent and broken, cheap gilded tin. I flattened it gently, and pressed it into my shirt pocket. I put the solitary horseshoe there with it. All the while, smoke traveled through the bedroom, and I wondered if it was from the forge. There couldn't be this much smoke from a single chimney.

The End of the Sentence

I should have spent more time in the library, Lischen was right. What did I know of the first of November? Nothing. Why were all the weddings this day? I'd assumed I'd have daylight to see by. I'd assumed Dusha would be released into the morning sun, but of course a prisoner would be released the moment the new day came, not hours after. He was free, and they would want to be free of him.

When I stepped out onto the front porch, I could see where the smoke was coming from. I marveled there wasn't more of it.

Fires all around the property line, bonfires, controlled. As far as I could see, there were stacks of wood silhouetted. I could see shadows of people at the edge of the flames, black figures, watching, milling about, and the sky was heavy with smoke.

The tree stump before the house was no longer a stump. A tree stretched its branches, each one covered in leaves. I looked up at the fruit ripening there, a harvest far out of season, peaches and plums, apricots, nectarines from a single tree. All of them so heavy they could have fallen from the branches and exploded on the ground. There was a deep sweetness coming from the earth, and the boards of the porch creaked beneath my feet, feeling live as the tree did, as though the house was likely to grow leaves of its own.

In my pocket, Hew's shoe pressed and thumped, skittering against my fingers, almost playfully.

There was another light, far off on the road. Two small yellow lights, like lanterns, moving slowly, strangely, swinging and bouncing. Was someone walking? Flashlights?

No, I realized, placing the sound. That was a car coming, and not a modern car. It sputtered, buzzing like something alive and wounded. It twisted slowly down the road from town, circling past the bonfires of my invisible neighbors. It was coming from the west.

I looked at my watch. Three-thirty. I'd lost hours in the preparations.

To the property's edge, that's what Chuchonnyhoof had promised. I thought about Row. He'd never wanted to be a princess on Halloween. He'd been a goblin. That had been his costume, a grey sweatshirt, heavy and hooded, and pockets full of bartered sweets. He was afraid of wearing a mask. The most he'd consent to was a swipe of green below his eyes, goblin paint, and all night he'd ride my shoulders as though I was a horse. That was a real memory, that was true.

"Slower, horse," Row's voice said in my mind. "Run slower." His small hands reaching around my face to feed me candy.

The shoe wrapped around my fingers, warm metal, and I felt comfort from the strangeness of everything. I could see smoke coming up from the forge too, not lit by me. Smoke and dry dust, red metal. I could taste the iron in the air, along with everything else. My face smarted, stung by it.

Maybe this would be my last night on earth, this cold, this smoke, these lights.

The car came spinning over dirt, past the place the truck had been. The bonfires were high, and so I saw it too, the outlines of a vehicle decades out of date, and carrying a heavy weight. The car rattled and moaned over the ruts in the road. I couldn't see into its windows.

A figure passed before me, and I looked up, startled, to see Ralph, his white hair swept back and twisted into braids, his clothing entirely different from the red t-shirt and jeans I'd seen him wearing before. He wore an old-fashioned apron made of worn black leather, over a white shirt like my own, but less fine. He looked at me and smiled.

"You wouldn't think I'd let you do this alone," he said. "You're no blacksmith."

"I'm not," I said. "But if I'm not the smith, what am I? This is my forge."

Ralph looked at me as though I was a fool.

"You're the groom now," he said.

There was still time to run, I thought, still time to flee this thing I'd let find me. I'd run before.

"This is your wedding night, Malcolm. May you have heaven in your heart. You're getting someone who wouldn't take me, nor anyone else. She's been waiting for a match, to take her hand in his. She's part of the town, and now you will be too."

Lischen walked out of the dark, her hair streaming behind her, her dress white and perfect as the nightdress I'd seen in the vision. Her feet were in boots. She was both ethereal and ferocious, but when she looked at me, I saw nothing but vengeance. Her teeth were bared. The berries, I thought, the offering, and there they were, in my hand, the beautiful basket from the hall.

Lischen looked at me, her composure broken for a moment. "Did you bring this to hurt me?" she asked.

"I would never want to hurt you," I said, still missing things. Still not understanding. "They're for you. From the house."

She raked her fingers over the basket, touching each woven twig as though she knew it.

"Yes, the house would give me this again. The end of the harvest," Lischen said. "The offering. Don't think I'll do your bidding for these, Malcolm. These are only the tradition, not everything."

"I give them to you," I said again. "They're a gift."

Lischen looked up, her face flaring.

"This is not about love," she said.

"This is about something else," I said. I felt tranced, like I had the moment after the accident, Row in my arms, heavy mind, racing heart. I took a berry, and looking at me, she took one too. She pressed it into my mouth, and I tasted it, sweet and overripe, too much and not enough. I wanted more even as I wanted to spit it out.

I pressed a berry to her lips, and felt them open, a strange feeling, like feeding a mare a sugar cube, and then that feeling was gone.

"This is about everything else," she said, looking at me with her golden not-horse's eyes.

The car came to a stop fifty feet from me, at the edge of the property that abutted the road, its headlights bright and yellow as Lischen's stare.

"They say on this night," Ralph said, rolling up his sleeves to reveal arms startlingly muscular, "the dead can walk. Ione is out to dance on these grounds with those they've loved and lost. Every year we do it, but this year is stronger than it's been in a hundred years and more, not since my grandmother's time. We've been waiting, Malcolm, for the end of the sentence."

"They say on this night," said Lischen, "the dead can talk. There are dead I want to talk to. And there are those who should be dead, and aren't. This is a wedding of the should-be-dead, Malcolm. I'll take your hand in mine, if you'll take mine in yours."

The shoe thumped, once more, in my pocket. "I—"

The door of the car opened with a crash and a clap, and a voice called out over the crackle of the flames, through the smoke and night moths, over the cry of a coyote somewhere far out in the hills.

"Malcolm," called the voice, gently, sweetly. "Malcolm."

20.

I'd been expecting a monster. Dusha Chuchonnyhoof the murderer, Dusha Chuchonnyhoof the Ironhide, Dusha Chuchonnyhoof the goblin made of rust and hooves— but he'd always been a monster.

"Malcolm," he called again, his voice gentle, a parent reassuring a child of the safety of the darkness. I walked towards the car.

When I saw his face through the smoke, he did not look like a monster. He didn't look like a man. He looked broken.

I looked into the car, and saw the prison warden, looking not at me, nor at his passenger, but straight ahead.

I could smell the iron and the corrosion, the rust that had turned his skin to red. It had crusted the beds of his fingernails, and lined his eyes, weighting the lids. He moved as if his bones were knives, carving his flesh from the inside, slowly, and too carefully. He picked up his feet as if the earth burned him.

His shadow, rising in the firelight to twist in the night and the smoke, did not match the rest of him, and I heard the townspeople around me, all the people I didn't know. Gasps and whispers. No one screamed.

I looked down at his feet. Hooves, yes, at the bottoms of his pants, and the thinnest layer of metal beneath, broken in places, hands too old to carry their burden. The hooves were black and dusty, like old wrought iron, or feet belonging to an animal near dying, and I thought again of my grandmother, her hands fixing the goats, but there were always some goats that had started on their way to death. She'd let those go. 'Too old a thing for fixing,' she'd said.

I could see centuries on Chuchonnyhoof's skin, and on the cracked horns that curved from his forehead. From one angle, I saw them. From the next, gone. The shadow showed the truth, and had I seen him only in that form, I would have fled. Here, though, in front of me, was a ruin, a man made of rust.

The only thing unruined was his eyes, nothing like anything else I'd seen in the world. It occurred to me that that was because they weren't from it. Milk-blue opals, strange, bright and tender, lined in that rust.

I nodded at him. "Welcome back, Mr. Chuchonnyhoof."

He smiled at me, a slow, grinding stretch of his skin. "Thank you, for that. Will you give me your arm? I am not as well as once I was, and the way is difficult."

He held out his hand.

I looked back. Ralph stood at the side of the house, near the door to the smithy, arms folded across his chest, hair silver in the light from the bonfires. Lischen stood next to him, mouth dark from the blackberries. In the light, the juice looked like blood.

I looked at the things that had started to rise from the earth, white trails of nothing, people in long dresses and short coats, a feather headdress, a wide-brimmed hat, all made of light and mist, bending around the fires, bowing, kneeling, circling.

The world of the quick had pressed itself hand to hand with that of the dead.

I imagined their graves, between the town and my land. The people, the living, fed the fires with wood they'd hauled from elsewhere. Far out in the sky, above all this, I could see the stars, but it was as though I was seeing them through netting. I thought of costumes. I thought of sweatshirted goblins and chiffon dresses. I squinted into the mist, hoping, but Row wasn't there.

Veiled in smoke, the people of Ione danced with their dead, and spoke to them.

There were dead I would give everything I had to speak to again.

Instead, I gave Chuchonnyhoof my arm, and staggered from the weight of him. Whatever he'd been before, he was iron now, almost entirely. We walked slowly, dragging through the grass, a bridal procession to the waiting priest, the watching bride.

"I know some of what you have done for me, Malcolm. I know that you have tried to care for the place. I am grateful." Chuchonnyhoof's voice was sweet and gentle. No thickness, no grinding of rust.

His fingers, where he clutched my arm, left red streaks on my jacket. "The place is mine," I said. "Better to fix what I can."

Chuchonnyhoof stumbled, nearly going to his knees, and I felt the strain along my side as I heaved him back up. His hand was rough, and snagged at my palm.

I turned my head, hearing the sound of soft hooves, and saw a herd of ghostly horses rising from the property line, unfolding their limbs, white and silver, circling the land, weaving between the smoking stacks. At their head, a mare of bone, haltered in ribbons of red.

"The mare's walk," Chuchonnyhoof said, his voice catching. "The *Láir Bhán*. Guised to bring fortune. A hundred and seventeen years since I've seen one."

I looked closer. Some of the horses weren't horses, but women, the horse forms transparent around them. They moved as though they were a single thing, a many-bodied ghost marching between the fires, around the families.

Lischen looked out at the procession, her face lit with longing. She turned to descend the stairs to the smithy, Ralph behind her.

Chuchonnyhoof's and my progress was slower. Each step deliberate, each movement an entire tick of the clock. The heat grew greater as we descended, the forge waiting in readiness.

"Have you enjoyed living in Ione?" Chuchonnyhoof asked.

"Enjoyed it?" I asked.

"Has it been a good place to live? Would you make your home here? Will you stay?" he said, and looked at me. "At the homestead?"

"Yes," I said at last. It was mine. I felt a claim on it.

"Good," Dusha said, and nodded. There was a snap, and he stumbled, hand clutching at my sleeve, then fell. Thumping against the walls, the lights shuddering from the impact. I ran after him.

He pulled himself up, half-leaning, half-sitting. Blood, a thicker red than his rust-stained skin, trickled from his temple, and his left nostril.

"My shoe," he said.

His right hoof was still shod, though it seemed only hope held it on. The left hoof was bare, and ragged.

The shoe, snapped in two, rested above us on the stairs, and Chuchonnyhoof's left leg was no longer human. It was hide, bristles of coarse fur like wire, the leg of an animal, a tremendous one. A beast. The hoof was split to the quick, and I could see the pain of it, the blood there too. As I watched, the transformation progressed, moving up Chuchonnyhoof's body, and I felt him getting heavier still. The stairs groaned beneath us. I stared at him, his skin darkening, his body larger than it had been. There was something indistinct about his edges, something that twisted up from his spine and then was gone, and his face shifted and then became his again. There was a raw sound, something ripping inside his body, and then he coughed blood, a hissing cough like a fox barking after prey.

"Hurry," he said.

"You get the shoe," Lischen said. "I'll get him."

She pulled him from the ground as if he were nothing, and carried him. They continued down the stairs.

The horseshoe was worn, in some places as thin as paper, and cold. The detail of the fingers near gone, it could have been anything woven together in that shape. On the inside, it was corroded with rust.

Red streaked the white of Lischen's dress, and her eyes glowed as bright as the flames in the forge, her mouth black and bloody from the berries. I could still taste the tartness of the fruit on my breath. She carried him as though he was nothing.

Ralph had gripped Chuchonnyhoof's other leg, and was pulling the remaining shoe loose with pincers. Chuchonnyhoof's shadow hulked behind them, huge and lurching, the darkness beginning to match the man. As I watched, the shadow drew a claw across Chuchonnyhoof's jawline.

"I need that one, too," Ralph said.

I placed the pieces in his hands, and he tossed both shoes into the forge. The smoke rose, white and thick.

"The bone fire is lit," Chuchonnyhoof said. I couldn't bear to look at him, his pain, and then I saw Lischen remove something from around her shoulder.

The silver bridle. Chuchonnyhoof nodded at her, baring his teeth.

"Yes," he said. "Yes. That is necessary. Thank you."

I saw her change for a moment, her hair too long, her body too large. She fit the bit between his teeth, and laced the silver around his head, and his shadow tossed and reared up, but she held tight to the reins. The bridle calmed his body. The shadow stilled, and Chuchonnyhoof stilled as well.

Hew's shoe thumped against my chest, against the little crown that was still there, over my heart. Once, twice. Then a third time. That was when I heard the footsteps reverberating down the stairs. Clanging and echoing in parade, louder than the ghosts outside, louder than the ghosts inside.

All of the paired shoes from the closet upstairs. This time, not empty. This time, this night, was when the dead of Ione could return, though they wore their hands as horseshoes.

They came down the stairs, a woman with Lischen's mother's face. Her father. Millers and Marches, all the names from the contracts, the watercolor-portraited, the locks of hair twisted together, two slender women, and last of all, unshod, a woman with silver braids around her head, and an apron made of black leather. No, not leather. A blacksmith's apron made of dark. I looked at her pale arms, her pale face, all of it shining with a light that came not from the sun or moon, but from under the earth. It was the phosphorescence of a cave, or of the things deep down in the ocean.

I looked at what dangled from her own hand. A smith's hammer. So Dusha had brought his dead here tonight too.

I wondered about the other dead. About Olivia Weyland, who was a ghost of the house. Were they here as well? About my dead, my Row. He was mine, but he was not Ione's, and this was not my place yet.

I took Hew's shoe from my pocket, and set it upon the anvil. There was no ghost for it, no one to wear it. It was alone, thumping.

Lischen looked away from it. "The witnesses have arrived."

"Do you both come here freely, and of your own volition, with the intent to bind yourself in this place?" Ralph asked.

"There is supposed to be love," I said, remembering the instructions. "For the binding to work."

Lischen knelt in front of the anvil, her white dress foaming around her. She laid her hand across it, and looked up at me. I thought of her weight in the bed behind me, thought of her smell. Thought of her teeth against my back, the feel of them not tearing at me, though she'd torn at Michael Miller. I thought of my own broken history. Who was to say which of us was worse?

Lischen tossed her head, shaking her hair loose from the silver threads that I now saw bound it. "Am I not something you could love?"

"Will you give her your hand," Chuchonnyhoof said, his voice stretching around the silver in his mouth, "and place it in hers, knowing what will happen?"

Ralph held a hammer in his hand. A pein, I remembered. On the anvil, a chisel. I imagined the strike, the chisel against my skin, then through it, separating bone from bone. I looked at an empty shoe, and at a woman who had mourned her child, two lifetimes and a day. No one ever died from grief, but there were those who lived with it.

"I will."

"Then that is love enough," Chuchonnyhoof said, sagging against the wall, wincing. Blood ran from the corners of his mouth, the drops falling to the floor. Beneath his hooves, the ground clattered with iron nails. "Let the contracts be signed and let the remunerations be written."

We signed our names and wrote our wishes on the papers. Ralph picked the brand out of the coals of the bone fire, and pressed it to the pages. C&W. The paper did not burn, but the smell of iron thickened.

I heard metal, scraping and grinding behind me. The forge, I thought. It would be hot. And it would be pain. Lischen, though, had survived it once before, and she was here again, a willing bride, offering her right hand this time. Her left had already been taken.

"You go first," Lischen said.

"No," said Chuchonnyhoof. "Together. I am, as I said, reduced." His voice was scarcely a voice now. A rasp.

Shaking only a little, I knelt over the anvil across from Lischen, and took her hand in mine. I looked at the faces of the ghosts, standing witness. All of them looked at me, except one.

That ghost rolled her sleeves from the wrist, pushing them up her arms. That ghost looked only at Dusha. Abigayl. For a moment, he looked back, and I saw his eyes close. When they did, the room flinched with him. I looked at the hooves and saw them splitting further, peeling back from his bones.

"Speak your wishes," Ralph said. He placed the chisel against my skin.

My hand clenched around Lischen's. As I clasped it, I felt in her palm the lone shoe. I pressed it into mine as well, hard between our hands. It was comfort, even if neither of our ghosts walked here. I felt the air shift as Ralph swung the hammer back. We spoke together.

"My son."

"He will return when I do," Chuchonnyhoof had written. The dead were here, and they were watching, and what was pain before that chance?

The pein fell, and I heard a howl, a roar, a churning like something ripping from the earth itself.

I felt the press of a roomful of ghosts against me, felt them holding a hand that held onto nothing. Pain, white-hot, large enough to block out my vision, my nerves screaming up my arm, a thousand ants, needles and trees falling, screaming pin-toothed animals, stampede, box canyon, ropes and knives. Sacrifice. Smoke, and the scent of a bone fire. Shapes and the shadows and rust and iron. Burning and burning and burning.

Then the cedar and silver scent of Lischen, and something cooler, too. Rain beneath the smoke, moss and darkness. Iron, and the dust-spice sweat of horses.

I opened my eyes, and looked down at my hands. Around my left wrist, a thin band of silver. Clasped hands, holding onto each other, never to let go. Lischen's back was to me, her head bent, and her thick black hair streaming over her shoulders. Ralph was kneeling at the unlit forge, searching for something in the ashes.

"Has something"—my voice cracked, rusty in my throat. "Is everything all right?"

"There are no new shoes," Ralph said. He stood by the forge, coated to the elbow in ash. I could see Abigayl there too, standing in the forge itself. She had something in her hands.

"I did not intend there to be. The end of the sentence has come and gone, and I am ending too. There is no more of me, or not enough. It is time for me to die." Chuchonnyhoof's shadow had fallen over him like a blanket, enfolding him in dark.

Abigayl opened her hands and showed what was in them. Two shoes. Mine and Lischen's. For a moment I saw the fire light again, a ghost fire this time. She tossed the shoes into it, and they were gone.

The ghosts no longer stood witness. All of the paired horseshoes were turned over, face down. Empty. Quiet.

"Malcolm," Lischen said, her voice changed from the voice I knew. It was softer. "Malcolm."

In front of Lischen, the rush basket from the house. In the basket was a black-haired boy. He smiled, and the corners of his lips curved up like Lischen's, but there was my dimple on the side of his mouth. I felt for the crown that had been in my pocket, but it was gone.

The skin of his left hand was silver, but where it met his arm, there was gold.

"Was this," I swallowed past the lump of wanting in my throat, "expected?"

"Better," came Dusha's voice, out of a corner that no longer was part of the room, "to fix what you can."

I could just see him, those eyes like sky breaking from the edge of a storm. The shadow was all around him now, and in the shadow, I could see other eyes glowing.

"A child is not like a shirt, to be changed out when torn," Lischen said, but her hands were tight on the boy, holding him, and he cooed.

"No," said Dusha. "A child is a child. This child is his own."

The baby's silver fingers stretched, and grasped Lischen's hair. The baby touched my face.

"This doesn't mean you're forgiven," Lischen said. "This doesn't mean I forget what you are, what you were, what you did, what you broke, who you hurt."

She walked across the room, and into the shadow like it held no fear for her. She leaned in.

"Still," she said. Hisses and cries, howls from the darkness. She took his hands in hers, (were they hands? They were not, but she held them as though they were) and kissed Chuchonnyhoof, hard on the mouth. His eyes stayed open as she did it. I saw them go liquid, saw a tear run down his wasted face. Blood ran from his lips when she pulled away.

For a moment, watching them, I thought it would be like a fairy tale. The princess kisses the monster, and then he's no longer a monster. Happily ever after. But Lischen stepped back, and Chuchonnyhoof's eyes closed.

Ever after.

The last thing I saw before the dark became a bend in the wall again, before the floor became stone, was Abigayl rolling down her sleeves, and stepping into the shadows, her hammer in her hand.

Then it was dawn, and it was the first of November. We walked up above the earth to find the marks of hooves and claws all over the frosted ground.

21.

not all of the magic disappeared after that. The dishes still washed themselves, and there was usually a woman's voice, low, singing love songs as they did. Meals were no longer cooked, but occasional elaborate desserts showed up. Birthday cakes once yearly. Lights glowed in the hallway. My torn shirts were mended.

The blackberries were still in fruit, out of season.

I didn't know who had stayed and who had left. It bothered me some, but then, I'd never really known whom I'd shared the house with in the first place.

I've had a telephone line installed. My family knows where I am now. The car needed work, but the mechanic did it, and at the end, the nest in the ceiling yielded fledglings who took flight when I opened the door to drive it for the first time.

Sean goes back and forth, one week at my place, one week at Lischen's. Sometimes I stay at her place, too. The silver on his hand has crept up a bit. It's just past the bracelet of clasped hands Lischen made for him to wear so he'd have one like ours. Maybe it will keep going, maybe it won't. The line of gold at the edge of his silver is bright enough that it could be real, something more than the remains of a gilt crown worn by a princess and by a goblin both.

There was one more letter. It came the day after the anvil marriage, after Sean's birth and Chuchonnyhoof's death. It was left in front of the door, and there were violets, gathered in a bunch, with it.

November 2

Dear Malcolm,

This is the last time I will write to you. I still hold out hope of Heaven, and I pray that's where I'll go.

The Catholics call today the Feast of All Souls. I never held much with their incense and their saints, but I do like the idea that today, we think on our dead. We remember them all, not just the good ones.

I told you before that no one ever dies of grief, but I think I was wrong. I think that Dusha Chuchonnyhoof died of grief. Maybe he deserved to, maybe not. I won't claim to be the judge of such things.

You can choose to die too, Malcolm, quick or slow, and I can't say as anyone would blame you. Or you can choose to live and fix what is broken.

Nobody who hasn't been hurt can work a miracle.

Yours,

Olivia Jones Weyland Chuchonnyhoof

It is said that too much iron in the soil poisons the ground. I can't imagine how much iron was in Dusha Chuchonnyhoof's body—an unbearable amount, I think. But things bloom over his grave—wild mint, and violets, and a tree with different fruit on every branch.

It was Lischen who made the marker, one day in the spring. Simple, Dusha's name. A horseshoe above it.

Below it, the words:

'Embrace me then, Ye hills, and take me in'.

Acknowledgements

Our gratitude to Bill Schafer for commissioning this novella over convention cocktails at ConFusion, as well as to Yanni Kuznia, Geralyn Lance, and Josh Parker, and to John Scalzi who formalized our contract written on skin by photographing and tweeting it. Also to Joe Monti, who handled the more traditional aspects of contract negotiation.

China Miéville for editing, strong tea & the idea for the prison scene; Olivia, who used to live in Maria's Brooklyn apartment and gets heaps of letters from prisoners who never knew her; the Oregon Historical Archive and Old Oregon Photos for introducing us to the work of Walter Bowman, and his 1890 portrait of a very small Native American boy with a prosthetic hand; Lischen Miller's 1899 Oregon ghost story, "The Haunted Lighthouse," from which the iron door comes; and Maria's dad, Mark Bryan Headley Sr. from whom she inherited the 200-year-old Headley family anvil.

In addition to those credited above who played a part in commissioning the novella, and who offered bits of reality far stranger than fiction, Kat would like to thank Sarah McCarry, for telling her she looked forward to meeting her monsters, and her Mom, Rebecca Howard, who provided food and sanity during a week of this novella's writing.